Surviving Spirits

by:
Andre Stefan

Motivo Publishing Company
Phoenix, Arizona

Surviving Spirits

by:
Andre Stefan

Published by:
Motivo Publishing Company
Phoenix, Arizona

Library of Congress Control Number: 2002112440

Copyright 2003 by Andre Stefan
ISBN: 0-9649210-3-0

Acknowledgments

I wish to thank several people who have impacted me in writing and finishing this book. First and foremost, God; without Him, nothing is possible. To my wife, the other person who shares my spirit, my love, my faith and my life; and who never once doubted that I couldn't do anything I set my mind to; thank you honey. To my son, the best gift God and my wife have given me. I couldn't ask for a better child. To my mother, for believing in me and making me feel like I could do anything from the day I was born and to my father, I know he is proud of me, as I am of him. I love you both. To my sister-in-law; this book wouldn't be complete without her part; To my brothers and sister and their families, just for loving me.

A special thank you to Matilda, who encouraged the writing of this book. And to the many special people, each hand selected for their unique individual spirits; their honesty as special editors made it all final; And to the person who believed in me as a boy and young adult, the memories of celebrating Mass with him will forever remain close to my heart, I miss and love you Father Steve.

Thank you one and all.......

Andre Stefan

Chapter One

The Dream

January 15, 1996 - 4:20 A.M.

*Outside was a restless night. The kind of evening that made every-
thing transient. The trees swayed, bushes rattled, dogs barked, cats
meowed and night time birds piped against the prevailing howling
wind that crept out of nowhere. The kind of evening that the full
moon, visible as that as the sun, illuminated all around. Out in the
distance a car horn blared, a muffled siren was heard. On an
evening like this, nighttime noises were muffled and nightime
scenes were blurred. Over the horizon, a light shone. A bright light.
Then it disappeared. Clouds rolled in and made their rest in front of
the moon. The blackness of the night enveloped its surroundings.
No longer were the crickets chirping, no longer were the frogs
calling. The symphonic music the tree leaves made, conducted by
the wind, ceased. Silence. Darkness. The earth began to spin. First
to the right, then a halt. Then it spun to the left and halt. again. The
bright light shined out in the distance. Gone again. The earth spun
again. A little further to the right this time, a little further to left as
well. Then it stopped. There again, the bright light... then the pitch
darkness. There in the darkness something moved. Standing in the
middle of this vast darkness was a figure of a man. Standing
straight he was, strong in his conviction. Strong in his purpose. He
was not disturbed as he focused on the bright light that would come
and go in the darkness. He reached out with his right hand and his
lips moved, though no sound left his mouth. Around him the wind
howled and blew stronger than before. Noises racked through the*

5

air. The night has gone crazy. Complete and utter chaos surrounds him. The man holds his stature firm to the ground as the tornado-like wind tries to battle him down. The bright light flashed again. This time closer. With every flash of the bright light, the man was pushed closer to it. Then with a loud bang, the wind and noises stopped. The only sound heard was that of the man's heart beat in the night. As the man pulls his arm down, in the quietness of the dark, a vision appeared before him. A single white door stood... Unsupported by nothing but the darkness. The man stares trance-like at it, still holding strong. Then the door swings out towards the man and inside was complete darkness and sad muffled sounds were heard. It stands open there for a few seconds then it swings away from him in the opposite direction and the bright light that shone before was there. The man instantly looks down, but his eyes still gazes into the bright light. It quickly shuts. The door again swings out into the darkness and back the other way into the light. The door struggles with every swing as it were being pushed by forces that could not be seen. Immediately, the door battles against itself. Faster and faster the door swings to each side.... and in a moment's notice.. it stops, swung open to the darkness. The noises were louder, the cries even more distinct and sinister. Then BANG! The door swings with every might to the glowing side. It swings with such force that the door explodes. A strong gush of wind whirls out, the man is forced down onto his knees. He keep his eyes at the vision before him. The bright light envelops everything around him. The door fragments whirl past him as he tries to escape from being hit. It was then that he notices that the tremendous force of the door exploding had changed the door. Right before him; the bright light and a set of double doors are visible.The light is brighter than before but he did not find it uncomfortable to stare into it. As the man rises to his feet, he notices the peaceful breeze and the calming sense of extreme happiness that he felt. Just then, someone lightly touches his shoulder and calls out his name. He couldn't make out who the voice was, but he felt he knew......

-- Father Ignacio?, Father Ignacio, wake up. There's a telephone call for you. They say its important.

-- Thank you Sister, tell them I'll be there in a minute.

Father Ignacio, looked around his room. Still delirious to his everyday surroundings, he swipes his hand over his hair and yawns. He notices he is a bit drained from this wake up call; different than other times. Just then, Father Ignacio looked at his digital clock on his wooden desk that sat in the corner of his tiny bedroom that was too musty in the summer and too clammy in the winter. 4:32 AM. Who could be calling at this hour? What day is this?, Father Ignacio thought to himself. As he reached over for his robe, incremental pieces of memory from the dream he just had confused him. He knew he just had a dream but the only details of clarity that came to him were those of victory. He shook out his thought as he opened up the door to his bedroom and walked down the hall of the rectory. There Sister Angelica stood, with a cup of hot coffee waiting for him at the kitchen table. Father Ignacio smiled at her a smile that had seemed to have said, "thank you, thank you Sister. Where would I be without you."

Sister Angelica is a stout woman. A stern-looking kind of woman. A woman whose face looked liked she had just spent her last twenty years in a concentration camp. The kind of nun that would smack your hands with a ruler back in her teaching days, but the same nun who would make you feel loved by her caring words of affection when someone was hurt or sad. She is about 5'.3", and a little on the heavy side. Sister Angelica always said, 'God, would have to forgive me for how I love food." She always thought that she commits one of the deadly sins when she eats. I would always laugh with her as I tell her, that I am further in committing bigger sin and that I would be the first to ask for forgiveness when my judgement times comes. But there Sister Angelica stood in her robe and her hair tied up in a bun held up with what looks like paper clips and there aren't very many people who have seen her out of her habit and nun shoes.

But she took care of Father Ignacio, the Church, the offices, the rectory and all of the organizations. She was definitely the rock of this parish and Father Ignacio felt blessed that they were playing on the same team.

--Father, the telephone. They are waiting for you, she said.

--Thank you Sister and thank you for the coffee.

Sister Angelica turns and walksback down the hallway to her room, cup of coffee in her hand and a shuffle to her feet. Father Ignacio picks up the receiver, holds it close to his ear and takes a sip of coffee.

-- Father Ignacio here.

-- Father?

A distinct sniffle was heard on the other line. Father Ignacio could not make out who the person was apart from being female.

--Yes, this is Father Ignacio

--Father, I hate to wake you up at such a late hour. But my sister asked me to call. She said that you wouldn't mind.

--Oh, Maggie, yes. Is everything all right? Where is your sister? Is she all right?

~ ~ ~

Father Ignacio hung up the telephone, ran his fingers through his hair and brushed his brow. He took another sip of coffee as he sat there. He peered out into the garden of the rectory. He rose, cinched up his robe and walked out into the crisp air. Memories flooded his mind. Memories of when he first met Makaila. Memories of many talks, walks and counseling. Memories of the incredible story that unfolded before him. Memories of two spirits that survived.

"And how they survived," Father Ignacio said under his breath. He sat on one of the patio chairs and reached into his pocket. He stopped and looked around as to make certain that a certain someone was not watching. He pulled out a pack of cigarettes and lit one. He took a puff and filled his lungs with the smoke that ever was so wonderful, especially at a time like this. He looked around again, making certain that Sister Angelica was nowhere to be seen. Father Ignacio smiled as he thought, "Sister has nothing to worry about with

her love for food." Father Ignacio leaned back into his chair and took another puff from his cigarette. The smoke lingered in the air around him as he sat, contemplated, prayed, and conjured up his thoughts on this wonderful and spiritual intercession of God that he has been blessed to be somewhat part of.

Father Ignacio sat there in silence. He puffed on his cigarette and sipped his coffee. The morning was cool, the moon ambered a subtle light on the earth. His thoughts raced, then as quickly as they raced, they stopped. Parts of the dream that he had earlier, cluttered his mind. "A door?, why am I remembering a door?" Father Ignacio thought to himself. He tried to push the thought out of his mind and the harder he tried the clearer the remembrance of that dream came. "A door?", he thought again as he grimaced and shook his head. Finally, the memory of the dream no longer played in his head. He was now able to focus on that phone call. Father Ignacio lit up another cigarette knowing that if Sister Angelica were there he would be due a good scolding.

~ ~ ~

He started to recall the day he met Makaila. Almost five years ago. A day he can clearly remember. Father Ignacio was giving a lecture at the local university. It was a particular day. The day he met part of a pair of survivors. Not the kind of survivors you would immediately think of. Not airplane crash survivors, not cancer or fatal disease survivors, nor holocaust survivors. These were special survivors, survivors of spirit. And it was a true miracle and blessings from the Lord above that they have become these survivors. They have Father Ignacio's heart and their relationship as God's children developed uniquely. And it has been from the very start that God put them in each other's path.

The lecture hour was almost up. Makaila sat at the fourth row of chairs that lined the small multipurpose room. Makaila gazed at Father Ignacio's every move and swallowed every bit of information that uttered from his mouth. Father Ignacio was made to notice the woman in the fourth row throughout his lecture. He could not understand why, but he was to put the pieces together as time went on.

Makaila wore a white laced top and skirt. She has eyes of blue heaven and a face of a ceramic doll. Her blond hair, accessorized the rest of her being just beautifully. The instant bond that was created that day is one of another blessing. When the class adjourned, and while Father Ignacio was wiping off the blackboard, Makaila stayed behind. She slowly packed her things into her case, while the other participants scurried out the door. Father Ignacio felt compelled to speak with her, to know her, to support her and to be there for her. Why he felt this he would not know until a few months later.

--So, Makaila? Makaila is it?

Makaila was startled as Father Ignacio spoke to her. She was rising to her feet also feeling the strong connection to this man she only met a couple of hours ago.

--Yes, that's right Father.

Makaila's voice only complemented the rest of her spirit. It was a calming voice. A voice as angelic as any angel. And yet, her voice sounded troubled. Her face told an unattainable story. And her eyes, were full of the Lord's spirit, but even then, also confirmed that she has seen some horrific things in her life. A story she could not tell. A story she didn't even know the extent of yet herself.

--Did you like the lecture today? Father Ignacio asked.

--It was remarkable. I really enjoyed it, Makaila replied.

-- That's good, Father Ignacio answered. Will you sign up for the rest of the lecture series?

-- Yes, I believe I will, Makaila answered. Father, um, would you mind joining me for a cup of coffee if you're not too busy?, she continued.

Father Ignacio looked at his watch and at the wall clock that hung above the blackboard. He looked at Makaila and even though he had other commitments when he returned to the parish, he accepted.

-- A cup of coffee sounds good, Father Ignacio replied. "I am just about ready." Makaila smiled at him and continued to put her purse strap onto her shoulder. Father Ignacio shoved some papers into his briefcase and looked around to make certain that he didn't leave anything behind.

-- Ready for that cup of coffee?, he asked her.

Father Ignacio propped open the door and Makaila smiled. A certain sense of relief went through Makaila's body and mind. She just knew that this man would come in great need, but most importantly, a person who would believe her from something she yet not believed or learned herself. This felt good she thought. She felt safe. Father Ignacio felt that he himself would be put to the test, but confident that in the end, he too would survive the story yet untold.

They walked out of the building onto a main street. Mill House Road. A street often visited by college students and their friends. A street in the middle of a large city that seemed to be in a world of its own. Mill House Road hosted many bookstores, campus dorms, fast-food restaurants, a few retail shops and coffee houses. A perfect place to sit under a patio umbrella, drink coffee and carry a conversation. Often, you would see college students walk around with different color hair, clothes you would find at a thrift store, young adults on bikes, skates or on foot, congregating outside each building with blaring music, loud talk or laughter. Makaila and Father Ignacio walked along the sidewalk not saying much at first. They both were trying to soak this world before them in, even though they have seen it a dozen times before. Finally they came to a coffee house far at the end of the street. It catered mostly to a much quieter crowd. They spotted an open table outside near a fountain and near a row of purple and pink flowers. They sat. Immediately, a young gal approached their table and asked for their drink order and as immediate as she approached the table she vanished to retrieve their drinks.

Small talk was how their meeting started. Makaila asked how long Father Ignacio had been a priest, what parish he worked at and the usual customary small talk inquisitions. Makaila mentioned that she herself worked as an adjunct facilitator at the university and had a twin sister. Eventually, small talk reverted to both of them noticing how much they had in common when it came to music, movies and the like and it wasn't long before smiles and laughter emitted from their table as they exchanged stories of their perspective lives. Before they could tell, they both realized they had just had three cups of coffee and two hours had gone by. When the inevitable silence came at the end of what they thought was their conversation, they both settled comfortably back into their chairs. Silence was visible between the two.

-- Makaila, I sense that you want to tell me something.

-- I sense that as well Father, but for the life of me, I don't know what. All I know is that I am supposed to be right here, right now. Words want to come out of my mouth and my mind has no idea what they are. And Father, I'm afraid. I'm afraid of something I cannot describe, or tell. I sense that something wants to be said and I don't know where to begin.

Father Ignacio took a sip of his coffee, lit up a cigarette and leaned further back into the chair. He looked at Makaila with compassionate eyes and smiled a strong smile.

-- Well then, we'll just have to start at the beginning won't we? *As it was in the beginning is now and ever shall be.....* Isn't that what the Bible says? Father Ignacio asked smiling.

Makaila smiled as she leaned forward onto the table and Father Ignacio listened wholeheartedly.

It was a beautiful March day when Lalee was admitted into the hospital for the births of their twins. Jack, her husband stood by her the whole entire time during the admitting procedure, and the look of pride on his face was more than those regular father-to-be's. There was an extra step of pride when he marched. Twins... He couldn't believe it. A few months ago, Lalee wasn't too keen on the idea of having children, but Jack insisted that it would be better for them to grow up together and not alone. Lalee did finally accept the idea and she also accepted that she was to give birth to two babies. Lalee felt particularly chosen and a gleam of sparkle was in her eyes, after all, she sort of knew she was to have twins one day. In her hospital room, Jack helped Lalee into her hospital gown as she prepared for the delivery of their special gifts.

-- Come on Lalee... Jack said in his stern voice. "Get into bed," he continued as he swatted Lalee on her behind as she was climbing into the hospital bed.

-- Jack, cut that out now, Lalee insisted.

-- You know I can't help it, Jack replied. You know you are as beautiful as that day I met you on that bus stop in Palm Springs.

-- Yes, I know and you're as handsome as that day you stood there in your military outfit...... before you left me that is, Lalee teased.

-- But I married you first before I left to war, Jack replied.

-- It's a good thing you came back in one piece or even alive, Lalee continued.

-- I had to come back for my girl, the most beautiful girl ever, Jack answered as he leaned down and kissed her passionately.

Lalee was a beautiful woman. Smart, gifted, talented. That kind of a classy woman next to Marlene Dietrich and Kathryn Hepburn. The kind of beauty that classic movie stars were made from. And Jack had come along and rescued her.

Lalee didn't have a relationship with her own mother since the death of her father when she was only eleven years old. Since then, things between her mother and herself had deteriorated and even though Lalee was as smart and gifted as she was, she always had a weak spirit. Finding Jack was going to be the start of a new life, a new chapter in her book and away from her mother. Maybe it was because of the death of her father or maybe because she was an only child, that the bond between her mother was really never established. But Lalee never imagined the life she was going to lead. Never in her wildest dreams was she to even fathom what life would be in store for her in the years to come. Her life would be hard. A life unbelievable. A life full of conse-quences to actions and actions to consequences. Up to this point, apart from the death of her father, she finally felt free when Jack came along, but having to stay with her mother in Palm Springs after her wedding, almost crushed her and she really never forgave Jack for that.

-- Jack? Did I ever tell you the dream I had when I was 17?, Lalee asked.

-- Yes Lalee you have.

-- Can you believe it's coming true? Lalee said excitedly. "What do you make of that?"

-- All I know is that we are going to have some special girls. Jack said.

-- I can remember that dream as if I just had that dream last night. Lalee said.

Lalee took on a somber look. The kind of look that hid pain in a person's life without revealing what that pain was.

-- I sure do wish my father was here, Lalee said sadly.

-- I know sweetheart, I know, Jack said empathetically.

Jack reached for her and kissed the back of her hand. They both sat there in silence, wondering what they each were thinking, waiting for whatever was going to happen next, to happen.

~ ~ ~

Lalee was 17 years old when she had a dream. She dreamt that she was at a church revival and Jesus was handing out five babies at the top of a hill. As Jesus was coming down, He handed three babies out to different women. When Jesus came to the bottom of the hill where Lalee was, Jesus said, "Would you take care of these two babies for me?" and Lalee said, "I will"... And now, Lalee felt she was preparing to give birth to those two babies.

~ ~ ~

Shortly after one o'clock in the afternoon, Maggie and Makaila were born. Lalee smiled as she lay there in that hospital bed as she watched her husband Jack shed a tear or two at the sight of his precious twin girls. Maggie was born first and a few minutes later Makaila was ready to face the world. These two precious gifts from heaven have already been chosen to parttake in a wonderful excursion throughout their lives. They will be instrumental in changing the lives of many who are in their presence, but most importantly, to lead the way for a soul back to God and away from the clutches of evil. These two little ones, with their blue eyes and hair of gold, their sweet innocence and their spirits of light will touch not only their own lives, but touch the lives and souls of those they will soon love.

~ ~ ~

-- So that's the day you were born. Father Ignacio asked.

-- Yes, almost forty-six years ago, Makaila answered.

-- And has life been good? Or did you not have the best of childhoods? Father Ignacio continued.

-- Oh no, Father, we had a great life. We had the picture perfect family. A house, a car, children and friends. We also had respect, religion, manners, clubs and vacations. The subtleties came after we were seven, Makaila said as she shifted in her chair.

-- Seven? What about the age of seven? Did that picture change, Father Ignacio questioned her.

-- Well, things started changing gradually before seven, but to everyone else, we had the perfect All-American life. Dad was a decorated veteran and mom was a concert pianist. What more could a family ask for?

-- What did you ask for Makaila? Father Ignacio asked.

-- To be loved..... Makaila said sadly.

-- Is that all you asked for? Father Ignacio pressed her.

Makaila's voice started to break and her blue crystal eyes began to water. Father Ignacio reached over and held her hand.

-- All I ever asked, and all that Maggie and I ever wanted was to be safe. Makaila said through broken tears. Aren't parents supposed to do that?

Father Ignacio reached into his black coat and pulled out some Kleenix and handed it to Makaila. Makaila wiped the tears that streamed down her cheeks.

-- You feel that your parents did not protect you? Father Ignacio said sympathetically.

-- No Father, they did not. And we feel that not only did they not protect us, but they put us in danger and I don't know what danger that would be. There are so many things in both of our lives that don't make any sense. Things we

19

are afraid of, things that we question and we don't know where to begin, Makaila continued.

-- When did those feelings start Makaila?

-- It started when our hair braids were cut off, Makaila angrily said.

Makaila slid back into her chair and wiped the tears from her eyes.

-- Braids? Father Ignacio confusingly asked.

-- Father, I hate taking this much time from you. I am sure you are needed elsewhere, Makaila apologetically said.

-- It'll be all right. Sometimes God gives us different paths in life and we as faithful children must be willing to change our plans, even if it means from day to day. So go on, as you were saying...

-- It all started when we were seven... Makaila continued.

Outside, the afternoon had passed and signs of dusk were present. More people were walking the sidewalks and the coffee house was getting a little busy. Father Ignacio called their server over for a fresh cup of coffee. Father Ignacio was as much willing to listen as much as Makaila wanted to talk. Even though he has heard similar stories, he knew that this one was a unique one, and God has it in His plan that Father Ignacio was there for a purpose. As much as Makaila didn't know what the story would entail, Father Ignacio knew that there was more that God wanted to reveal to him.

~ ~ ~

Lalee having twins was not an easy task for her. With Jack at work all day and Lalee at home all day with the twins, was a little too much to bear for Lalee. Postpartum depression played a major role in Lalee's deterioration on how she changed. But she managed as well as she could.

Lalee kept Maggie and Makaila in playpens and high chairs as much as possible. The twins were always so busy, always so creative and always so full of laughter. They smeared food on their heads and on their trays. Little did anyone know that they were being their creative selves.

Over the next two years, the twins did not stop. They had this special gift of being each other's playmate and they played and played. At one particular time, their grandfather came for a visit. The next day, pounding was heard in the early morning which woke everyone up. When the twins were in their "running and playing" mood, they would run from Lalee in different directions and there was their Grandpa, building a fence around the backyard for this reason.

These girls played everywhere and every time. They played in the garage and backyard in the summer and the basement and bedroom in the winter, and their creative juices were always flowing. If they were not building forts, creating plays, playing house with their dollies, or running around naked while Lalee scurried after them, they were bothering their neighbor. Their neighbor would always come down his tall ladder in a flash to little voices saying, "Misser Sodo, got a sucker?" and he always did. Mr. Soto was their first relationship with a safe person.

Their relationship with their parents was short of precious at this time. Makaila always felt close to her mother. Lalee would play with them by helping them wrap their dolls, and she sewed the twins clothes and made them each coconut bunny cakes and Easter egg hunts on their birthday. Lalee was very particular about manners and politeness from her Southern upbringing, and she was also very particular about honesty. The twins got a taste of that when one day the twins and Lalee marched back to a grocery store to return the Tootsie Rolls they had taken to feed their dolls. Lalee taught them many things thoughout their first six years. Lalee loved music and they would sing songs all year round and especially at Christmas. They would sing in the car when they visited their grandparents house once a month and they sang after dinner so they can get their two cookies. Lalee was especially delighted when Makaila played, "In your Easter Bonnet" on the piano. The twins always gave thanks to God at meals and had great manners when they were taught, *"this hand sleeps, while this one eats"* and the precious prayers every night as they kneeled in their pajamas at the foot of their bed.

They had what seemed the perfect life. They hunted for treasures in the alley, pulling their red wagon to show their mother what they had found. They took family vacations, cooked breakfast in the woods, went on hikes, built bridges, swung on vines, learned to swim, rode bikes and just had fun. Christmas at this family's house was a joyous time. Lalee and Jack put in a lot of time in decorating and creating a fantasy time for the both of them. They went to church every Sunday and the twins loved Sunday school. Makaila was destined at the age of five, when God touched her heart, when they sang, "Jesus loves Me," Makaila just knew that "me" meant her........ but all that stopped in what seemed one day.

Maggie and Makaila learned, as probably as soon as the womb, that they needed to care for each other. Even as babies, Makaila would often give up her toys to give to Maggie because she couldn't stand it if she cried. They both learned about love, nurturing, safe and unsafe people at this early age. They both knew that their relatives on both sides of their families were safe people. These relatives loved the twins and the twins couldn't wait to visit them again. Lalee and Jack also had another family as friends and their children and the twins acted more like siblings than friends or the other neighbor who would come and visit every night after dinner. She had a calming effect on Lalee who was always overwhelmed by her day and one day she stopped coming by. Makaila felt sad and an unsafe feeling came over her when that happened. Lalee was starting to describe their neighbors differently and negatively and always about the people that Makaila felt safe about.

Makaila recalls the one night when strange people came to the house and escaped to the basement with their mother and Makaila did not feel safe. She wondered where her mother had gone and why. These people were not neighbors or friends, Makaila just knew that these were not safe people. After that, Lalee was never the same. All the nurturing things Lalee did for her girls had stopped. She now had other interests, as she "whipped out the door to dancing lessons." The worst part is how their parents had gotten strict with them and bad spankings were part of their lives and they never knew exactly why they were being spanked. They only knew that Maggie was the scapegoat and the spankings got worse.

Makaila at such an early age felt that this was not "feeling" normal and despite the changes that were happening in their lives, she still loved her mother. Makaila still felt proud that Lalee was her mother. Makaila admired

23

her mothers movie star beauty and felt that she had the best and prettiest mom in the whole world. Maggie needed Makaila to be there for her and when the time came in their lives when school started for them, it was Makaila who hated leaving their mother and everyday Maggie would leave her school room and enter Makaila's room crying for a hug.

By the age of seven, safe people started disappearing from their lives, Lalee started having relationships with strange people and the spankings have gotten much worse. It was then that Maggie and Makaila put their dolls in one bed, crawled together into the other bed and held on to each other's night-gown. And in the morning they would wake up with soaked sheets and both of them sucking their thumbs. Little did they expect, for what they were about to learn about their past, the unbelievable memories they would both share as adults, the unrelenting horror they survived, that they would continue to hold tightly to each other's nightgown for many years to come.

Chapter Three

July 21, 1991 - 7:12 P.M.

Outside the Coffee House

Makaila had shut down from the woman that Father Ignacio first met a few hours ago. Makaila's retelling of her childhood had taken over and even though her childhood was a happy one, the outcome of her biography was even too much for her tell.This was obvious as Makaila sat there in that patio chair, with a different look on her face. The kind of look that made your skin crawl out of anger, the kind of feeling you get when you watch something or hear something that seems not so fair to the people it happens to. Father Ignacio read every language her body made as it said; "I can't go on any longer," and the ironic thing about it is that Father Ignacio had never met a stronger person. What kind of story weakens a spirit but strengthens a soul?" Father Ignacio thought to himself.

Father Ignacio knew, without knowing, that the worst was still yet to come and the worst will be the worst.

-- Makaila? Makaila? Father Ignacio called in a voice to have said, "You've said enough, don't let this story take you down."

-- Sorry Father. I just never told anyone this and it's hard. Makaila finally answered him.

-- Makaila, sometimes things that are hard for us are the best for us, Father

Ignacio counseled her. "Hard things in life make us stronger for the rest of our lives. And Makaila, you have a lot of life yet to go."

-- But it's not fair Father, it's simply not fair! Makaila stressed.

-- Everyone has a story Makaila. Some stories are harder than others, but everyone has one.

Father Ignacio knew that what he was telling her didn't matter much to Makaila. Father Ignacio's advice was only to bring some normalcy to Makaila's story, even though Makaila didn't believe so.... even though Father Ignacio didn't believe so.

As quickly as Makaila shut down with her story, she came up as quickly as that. She smiled at Father Ignacio. Her spirit awakened within her and her soul smiled through her eyes. Father Ignacio remarked again at the inner strength this woman had, and yet as Makaila's soul flourished, Father Ignacio's soul prepared to what seemed to be for a battle. A test of faith as you will, and Father Ignacio did not like the feeling. Father Ignacio questioned God's plan in this and that of Makaila's. Why had God placed this woman before him? What could he possibly do to ease the pain and hurt and fear of this woman?

Father Ignacio knew that his role in this was not just to counsel or to listen or to offer a shoulder. Father Ignacio believed that it would be more than that. And God made that decision without him knowing and what to expect from him. Father Ignacio's faith grew at this moment, something that he never thought and took for granted, but Father Ignacio put on his armor and received the test that would be the next five years of his life.

-- Father, I can not thank you enough and I feel so bad that I have taken up your afternoon.

-- Thank you Makaila, for sharing with me. I am blessed to have been available, Father Ignacio answered.

-- You know Father, I don't even know why I came today. I don't even know why I am telling you all this. I never invite strangers to coffee, and yet I feel as you and I are not strangers or have ever been.

-- Strangers are those you mistrust Makaila, that's what I believe anyway. Thank you for trusting in me.

Makaila's soul smiled as it heard every word that Father Ignacio voiced. Makaila thought to herself, "What a wonderful man. What a spirited man. Her soul felt loved by Father Ignacio's soul and Makaila knew at that instant that those two souls would bond.

-- Thank you again Father, I can not thank you enough. You have been more than kind to share your thoughts and help me to understand this, Makaila said.

-- Makaila, you know that this is not over. You have a lot more to say, a lot more that God wants you to know.

-- Yes, I know Father, and that frightens me, Makaila answered.

-- God, only reveals things to us when the time is appropriate and reveals only enough for that which we can handle at the moment. God's protection is upon us always, Father Ignacio insisted.

-- I hope so Father, Makaila said. "I still don't understand what I am doing here, why today, why you?" She continued.

Makaila started gathering her things, lifted from her chair and extended out her hand.

-- Father, I must not take anymore of your time. Can I call you again sometime?

-- I would be honored if you will. Father Ignacio said smiling.

After exchanging business cards, Father Ignacio stood up. Makaila saw the man from a different sight this time. Father Ignacio stood tall. He stood strong. And Makaila felt for the first time that she could too. Makaila, reached for her purse and strapped it onto her shoulder, she picked up her case with her left hand and stuck the kleenix Father Ignacio had given her into her right hand skirt pocket. The evening had come and the city lights blared against the sky above them. People were talking all around them and for the first time since they sat, they saw and heard life go on as usual. Funny how they both thought that no one was around this whole time that they had been speaking. It all seemed to have vanished away, like they were the only two in the midst of calmness. Father Ignacio extended out his hand as well and when their hands touched their souls jumped within them. Their souls were committed to each other from that point, committed to do battle against whatever was in store for them. Their souls recharged and the love that was sensed at that moment was that of God's love. Two people destined by God's intervention, two Christ-like people to make a difference in the world, two people who will show the greatness of faith, two beings that would become extraordinary friends, the essence of ultimate fellowship, friends for life, friends till death, friends..... forever.

Makaila turned to walk away. Her head held up high, her strength consumed by her smile as she walked strong against the moving bodies that had congregated around them. Father Ignacio stood there in the background as his soul silhouetted there against the night. He called out to Makaila.

-- Makaila!, Father Ignacio said in a raised voice.

Makaila turned around and looked at Father Ignacio. She noticed him smile, with the waterfall landscape behind him and his long black coat waving against his legs by the wind that had started out of nowhere. He stared at her for what seemed like minutes as she waited for him to say something.

-- God's trying to prepare you for something, Father Ignacio professed.

And with that Father Ignacio saw Makaila smile, turn around and continue walking as she disappeared from his sight into the crowd. Father Ignacio stood there for a minute as he watched the people close in like the closing of the Red Sea. He sat back down and noticed the almost cold air that surrounded him and the wind that started with no warning. He clutched his coat around his chest and reached over for a cigarette. He sat there, rewording, reworking, relistening to everything that he heard tonight. After that he knew that he was to embark on something scary, something horrific, something that was not of God... and the last words he spoke to Makaila rang out in his head, "*God's trying to prepare you for something...*" He looked up into the sky as he felt that those words were for him as well and he muttered under his breath, "*thy will be done...*" and he started praying, "*Our Father, who art in heaven.....* and Father Ignacio drifted into his prayer.

~ ~ ~

Father Ignacio walked around the house that sat at the corner of a street unfamiliar to him. He noticied the house with its huge picture windows, half brick and half wooden walls, standing almost at the top of the hill. He walked up to the front door. He questioned himself as to his visit there. Was it a marital counseling session? Or maybe it was a house blessing that he was asked to come and perform. He could not figure out why he was called to this home. He reached up to the door and he noticied that the door was wide open. He peeked inside and called out, "hello?", "Anyone home?" There was silence. The deafening sound of silence answered back as Father Ignacio was com-pelled to walk through the door. He stopped in the foyer that met him at the entrance. He walked past a room to the left what seemed to be the dining room. There was a setting for three persons. No one was around. He continued to walk through a carpeted room. Against the far wall was a brick inlaid fireplace. To the left of this fireplace were the picture windows he saw outside. On the opposite side he saw a wood paneled wall with a large picture of a little girl that seemed to have been painted years ago. The room felt warm and was bright with light. Father Ignacio stared at the picture for a long time, trying to read the girl's face. He sensed that the girl was sad and yet she smiled, almost a feeling of gloom and doom beyond that smiling face. "Is anyone here?"

Father Ignacio shouted out towards the room. No answer. He looked at the picture one more time, as he walked past it. He walked through a door into the kitchen. In the kitchen there was a foul odor. The air was thick, sticky and steamy. Father Ignacio felt a presence. He immediately grabbed hold of his crucifix he kept tucked into his shirt. There were no tables or chairs in the kitchen. No signs of anyone living in that space was visible. Father Ignacio heard some gurgling noises coming from a corner of the kitchen. The room became foggy. Light in the room was scarce even though the light from the burning sun was coming through the window. There in the corner stood a cast iron wood stove. On top of the wood stove stood a large pot. Froth rolled off the top edges of the pot and the odor even more foul than before. Father Ignacio held tighter to his crucifix out of instinct as his soul reacted to the presence in the room. Father Ignacio walked towards the stove. Slowly, scared and yet insisting in seeing what was inside the pot. He started reciting a prayer of faith, a prayer of command that whatever was present to be ceased, bound and returned to hell. Father Ignacio neared the stove. As he was about to peer in, a door behind slammed against it's hinges! Father Ignacio jumped and turned towards the loud sound.... nothing else was heard. When he turned back around to face whatever was present in the pot or near the stove, he was shocked to see... nothing. There in the corner of this kitchen stood a stove; newer in design. The sunlight from the windows rested on the floor and on the counter as the stream of sunray rolled across the kitchen wall. The kitchen was painted yellow and white hand-painted flowers were placed along the borders and certain areas of the room. Father Ignacio rested his grip on his crucifix as his soul resumed, waiting on guard. The foul odor had disappeared and the kitchen looked radiant as it should. Father Ignacio's heart returned to it's normal beating. He gathered his thoughts to what he just experienced and a sick feeling came over him. He mustered up his inner strength and once again he composed himself. What was the significance of that vision? What did it mean? What was going on in this house and why was he summoned to come here? Father Ignacio turned to ascertain that the vision he witnessed had not returned. He felt the need to continue through the house. He walked past the kitchen down a hall. Along the paneled walls of the hall were picture frames. Portraits of family, friends and loved ones he assumed. As he looked closer at the people in the pictures he noticied that the people's faces were blank. Where people's features would be, their eyes, nose and mouth, seemed to be airbrushed out. On the opposite wall were a set of two pictures. He recognized Makaila in one of the pictures. On the other picture, another woman who looked like Makaila. Father Ignacio was perplexed at what he saw. He was now confused and even more curious as his whereabouts. Father Ignacio continued down the hall. In the center of the hall was a door. It had an iron lock. Father Ignacio once again felt the presence of something evil. He held on tighter to his crucifix as he approached the door. As soon as he was within an arm's length from the door, the door swung open! Darkness poured out from it. Awful and sinister cries came from within and echoed through the hall. Father Ignacio could not make out what was down there. He couldn't see past the first two steps that obviously went down into a basement or cellar. Again, that foul odor was present. "*I command you in the name of Jesus Christ, Son of God, to cease and depart....*" Father Ignacio spoke in a loud voice. Cries got louder, the odor stronger, coldness filled the air around him. "*I command you in the name of Jesus Christ, Son of God....*" he repeated even louder. Demonic cries, demonic voices and laughter rose up from below. Father Ignacio trembled with conviction as he held tightly to his crucifix at the empty space before him. "*I COMMANND YOU, IN THE NAME OF JESUS CHRIST!!!!*" he screamed, sweat poured from his forehead as he recited his exorcism prayer. He reached into his coat pocket and fumbled for his Holy Water bottle. He opened it with one hand and his other hand held tight to the crucifix aimed at the opening of the door. He trembled with conviction, he shook because of the freezing air and he shuddered in faith as he sprinkled the Holy Water into the vast darkness. *"In the name of Jesus Christ...."* The door crashed closed and the force of it sent Father Ignacio flying as of something picked him up and hurled him into the air and landed him hard against the wooden floor. Father Ignacio laid still and after a few seconds he slowly opened his eyes. He found himself on the floor in what seemed to be a study. He rose slowly to his feet, noticied the sweat on his brow, his mussed hair. In his hands clutched tightly was the crucifix and the bottle of Holy Water. He looked around the room that was bright with light....empty within. The room had dark oak built-in book-shelves on all four walls. Suddenly a bright light came from behind him, Father Ignacio swung around.... and on the east wall, high above on the highest shelf was a single book. The book broke open with such might and the bright light exploded into Father Ignacio's face. He could not stare into the light, he fell to his knees, closed his eyes to restrain from seeing into it and Father Ignacio collapsed onto the floor.

Makaila bolted straight up from bed. Sweat poured from her forehead as she heard herself moan just as she was coming out of this dream. "Oh no, Fa-ther..." she heard herself say. She clutched her face with her hands and began to pray. She prayed in silence and then out loud. While she was praying she tried to remember the dream she just had. All she could remember was Father Ignacio's presence and she felt guilty of that. After she composed herself, she got up from her bed and walked into her living space in her tiny apartment. She reached for a drink of water. She knew that trying to sleep now was out of the question. As she sipped on her water, a part of the dream came to her, a book and Father Ignacio laying on the floor. She lay the glass of water down on her coffee table and reached for the phone. She picked up the receiver and was about to dial Father Ignacio's residence when she realized the time and that it was only a dream. She quickly hung up the telephone. She rose from her couch and walked over to her Spinit piano. She sat in front the black and white keys and began to play. She played like she never played before. She played for help and she played for protection and yet she played in thanksgiving and in praise. The evening ticked away with the subtle whisper of music in the air. The time was 12:42 A.M.

~ ~ ~

The rest of the evening after meeting Makaila for afternoon coffee had Father Ignacio's mind pre-occupied. Sister Angelica made certain that things ran smoothly at the Church while Father had a light supper and rested in front of the fireplace. He contemplated everything he had heard today from Makaila and he was convinced that he would help in any way he could. He felt that God would make certain of that as well.

-- Father, you should get some sleep now, Sister Angelica persisted.

-- No Sister, not tonight. There will be no sleep for me tonight. Something weighs heavy on my heart and soul. Father Ignacio said, without even looking up at Sister Angelica.

-- Can I be of any help to you Father? Sister Angelica asked.

Father Ignacio turned to look up at Sister Angelica. He rose from his chair from in front of the fireplace. He walked past Sister Angelica and stood next to her. He reached over and touched Sister's shoulder.

-- There is one thing Sister, Father Ignacio continued.

Sister Angelica, opened her eyes wider, knowing quite well that her devotion to God and to her committment as a nun, would come to be part of her night tonight.

-- When you retire into your room Sister, would you pray for me?

Sister Angelica, stood up straighter and held her neck and head up as if preparing for battle. She smiled at Father Ignacio and nodded.

-- Whatever you say Father, Sister Angelica responded.

Father Ignacio squeezed her shoulder as he walked to his bedroom. He flicked on the light that dimly lit up his room. He knelt on the kneeler in his room where a crucifix of our Lord hung. He heard Sister Angelica close her door to her bedroom as he heard her softly begin her prayer. Father Ignacio crossed himself, "*In the name of the Father and of the Son and of the Holy Spirit,*" as he started his vigil. Within seconds, a "thump" was heard behind him. He turned.... and on the floor beside his foot lay a book that had accidently fallen off the bookshelf. He picked it up, a book he never noticed before and placed it on his nightstand close to where he was kneeling. He began his vigil again as the night passed with the soft whispers of powerful prayers coming from the two rooms of this small church rectory. The time was 12:42 A.M.

Chapter Four

Monsignor Kealy

Two weeks had passed before Father Ignacio saw or heard Makaila again. In the past fourteen days, Father Ignacio had asked for strength, for power and had knelt in prayer. His soul was on guard and his conscience mind did not know why. In the course of meeting Makaila, he not once regretted or resisted his role in this path God has chosen for him. Father Ignacio felt that this was his destiny, one of the reasons why he was put on this earth, one of the reasons he followed his calling into the priesthood. It was times like this that he remembers his mentor. A good old Irish priest from Vatican I and old-fashioned in his ways, but Father Ignacio yearned for his wisdom, knowledge and just for his support at this moment. He can remember the countless nights that Father Ignacio and Monsignor Kealy would sit in his home, stay up to late hours, with drinks in hand, stale pipe smoke that bellowed in the air while the Irish one tickled the ivories in the sitting room. There have been many times when Father Ignacio was at a stand-still, a turnpike or even a fork in his non-secular world, where he would seek the advice of Monsignor Kealy and despite the differences in Vatican theories, their friendship were based on their kindred spirits. Just when Father Ignacio had no where else to turn, Monsignor Kealy seemed to always be there; And this situation was no different. Father Ignacio picked up the telephone one evening a couple of days ago...

-- Monsignor Kealy? Father Ignacio questioned.

-- Nacho, he said lovingly. "Thought you had forgotten your old friend here?"

Monsignor Kealy added.

-- Now Monsignor, How could I possibly forget you? Father Ignacio smiled through the telephone.

-- So how is my favorite Altar Boy?

-- Monsignor I am well... and how are you? Father Ignacio replied.

-- I am good. Thank God, Monsignor Kealy recited as usual. "But you are not pulling the cassock over my eyes. What is happening in your life that has your Rosary beads tied in a knot," he continued.

Monsignor Kealy had a way of saying things that would make any laymen, as well as those fellow priests who knew him, kind of wonder how he got away with this type of sacrilege..... if there was one. Maybe it could of been his many years of devotion to the Church or maybe because of his Irish ethnicity or maybe just because he was Ol' Monsignor Kealy. Nonetheless, his personality, his genuine love of people and his spirit made up for it.

-- Well Monsignor, I do have to see you today, Father Ignacio responded.

-- You do remember where I live don't you, Nacho? Monsignor Kealy asked teasingly.

Monsignor Kealy was the only other person apart from Father Ignacio's parents and relatives, that calls him by his nickname. And probably the only other person who can get away with it...and.... Father Ignacio in all honesty liked it.

It made him feel unpressured from being a priest, that facade of being in all control, that portrait of "specialness" by God Almighty above, and puts a reality check that he is "Nacho" first and Father Ignacio thereafter.

-- Shall I bring your usual order, Monsignor? Father Ignacio asked.

Monsignor Kealy took advantage of when Father Ignacio visited. Father Ignacio took special pride in bringing Monsignor Kealy his favorites things in life apart from God and the Catholic church.

--Now son, why else would I say that you're my favorite Altar Boy if it weren't for that, Monsignor Kealy jokingly said. "Be here promptly at 4:00," he continued.

-- Until then Monsignor, Father Ignacio said.

-- Until then and God bless, Monsignor added as they hung up the telephone.

~ ~ ~

Monsignor Kealy reached over and picked up his pipe. He took a couple of puffs from it as he slowly stood up from the winged back chair he was sitting on. His ailments of age were obvious as he walked ever so slowly to the bookshelf in the corner of his home. He pulled out an old blueish-grey photo album, with yellow-faded pages that hosted decades of memorabilia. Pictures of his mother's latest photo, pictures of himself early in the seminary, his ordination, a few friends from his mission work in Chili, Peru and the Philippines, and the many photos of his last parish he presided. He turned the book around,

---

dusted the dust off with his hand and returned to his chair. Monsignor Kealy leafed through the pages of his history and towards the last few pages, he paused. He smiled when he saw pictures of Father Ignacio as an Altar Boy, then when he was in the seminary and his ordination. Monsignor Kealy sighed in joyfulness, "such a good man he is," as he yawned and closed his eyes for an early afternoon nap.

~ ~ ~

Father Ignacio stepped out of the rectory and into the sultry air and bright sunshine. He was anxious to see Monsignor Kealy as it has been a couple of months he hadn't seen him. He could see Monsignor's face light up when he first sees Father Ignacio and the treats he would he be bearing. It has been an unspoken tradition that whenever Father Ignacio would visit the good Monsignor he would bring him a fast-food cheeseburger and a bag of his favorite pipe tobacco. Two things he shouldn't be doing per doctor's orders; but Monsignor Kealy was never one to follow rules, especially if they pertained to him. Father Ignacio drove along the windy roads to Monsignor's home left to him by his family's estate. Years ago it would have been considered out in the country and the nurses of his order worried that Monsignor would be secluded and too alone. Over the years, life and increasing population has filled in the many gaps and is now not so remote from civilization. On the way up, Father Ignacio could not help but to "walk down memory lane," from the first time he met then "Father Kealy" to the now elderly, retired "Monsignor Kealy."

And there was Monsignor Kealy, sitting on his front porch as Father Ignacio turned into the made-shift driveway up to Monsignor's home. Father Ignacio noticied how Monsignor Kealy had aged since the last time he visited. He grabbed the bags from the back seat of his car, as he dropped his keys into his coat pocket.

-- Nacho, my boy!, Monsignor shouted as Father Ignacio reached the steps to the front porch where Monsignor Kealy was sitting.

-- Monsignor Kealy, how are you sir?, Father Ignacio smiled. No, no don't get up, he continued.

-- Oh nonsense, Monsigner Kealy stammered.

Father Ignacio walked onto the crickety porch and watched Monsignor Kealy slowly inch his way up from his crickety rocking chair. Father Ignacio held out his hand. Monsignor Kealy pulled Father Ignacio closer to him and they hugged. Father Ignacio had always felt that Monignor Kealy was more of a father to him than his own father. In those troublesome years of teenage and adolescents where a son needs a father most in his life, Father Ignacio felt that his own father was not there available to him. He often felt that his father was threatened when Father Ignacio started the church as a young boy and it took Father Ignacio a long time to figure the reasons why. His father is that of the typical Mexican, macho man and "if you didn't spit, sweat and swear" you weren't a man, and Father Ignacio, for many years, resented this. It was Monsignor Kealy who taught Father Ignacio those things which are usually taught by one's father; but Monsignor Kealy taught him so much more than this; and for this, Father Ignacio was grateful.

Father Ignacio welcomed this embrace from Monsignor Kealy. What a feeling f a secure and unconditional love.

-- Nacho Nachito, let me look at you, Monsignor Kealy said as he held Father Ignacio at arms' length. "The priesthood has been good for you my boy," he continued.

-- Thank you Monsignor, you are looking great yourself, Father Ignacio said.

-- Well retirement does good for a body. Come, come sit down with me. I'll go get us a drink, Monsignor Kealy added.

Monsignor Kealy scooted off. The old screen door squeaked open as he disappeared into the house. Father Ignacio could smell the musty old smell of pipe tobacco in the air as he set the bags he had in hand down on the patio table. Father Ignacio sat next to Monisignor Kealy's rocking chair. As he sat he noticied that on the patio table lay Monsignor's things; a prescription bottle, his pipe and lighter, his Roman Book of Rites and underneath this book another book, with a binder that was quite familiar to Father Ignacio. Just as he was about to slide the Book of Rites out of the way to see the book underneath, Monsignor Kealy blurted something from inside the house. Father Ignacio stuck his hands in his coat pockets as he stood up and walked to the end of the porch.

-- I'm sorry Monsignor, Father Ignacio shouted. "I didn't hear you," he responded.

-- What I was saying was, "How was your drive up here?" Monsignor replied.

Monsignor Kealy stepped out onto the porch with a tray with two glasses that did not match and a couple of paper plates.

-- Oh, it was fine Monsignor, thank you.

Father Ignacio realized at this point that he didn't remember the drive up. He did know that his mind was occupied with thoughts of Makaila, his uneaseness with the situation and remembrances of Monsignor Kealy and himself many years ago.

-- Come sit down Nacho, Monsignor notioned to Father Ignacio.

Father Ignacio smiled at him as he fixed his thoughts onto Monsignor's hands. He could remember as a boy that Monsignor's hands to him were like Christ's. He can clearly remember how he fixated his eyes on every move Monsignor made when he was an Altar Boy standing beside him at the Altar while they celebrated Mass together. The feeling that Father Ignacio got when he saw Monsignor's hands come together in prayer and especially when he lay his hands over the Chalice at the time of consecration, was the same feeling he just experienced. Now, Monsignor's hands were little thinner, a little longer, and his veins a little bluer, but they still held the power he was invested with as a priest.

-- Now, my boy.... where are those burgers? Monsignor Kealy asked.

-- I have them here Monsignor and why do I feel I commit a sin whenever I bring these to you?, Father Ignacio added.

-- Oh nonsense Nachito, what do those doctors and nurses know anyway, Monsignor responded sarcastically.

Father Ignacio reached into the bag he had set on the table and took out the two fast-food burgers with cheese and gently placed them on each plate. Monsignor looked like a child as he unwrapped his cheeseburger. He unwrapped Father Ignacio's burger as well. He slid the plate closer to him and with a knife he delicatedly cut the burger in half and set each portion in such an art fashion on the plate as if he were serving prime rib. He slid the plate back to Father Ignacio only having done the same delicate carving to his own burger. He signed himself with Father Ignacio following.

-- *In the name of the Father, the Son and the Holy Spirit*, he said. *"Bless us oh Lord and this food, may it become for us a source of nutrition and bountiful health."* he prayed.

Monsignor Kealy held up his right hand as he made the sign of the cross over their plates and Father Ignacio thought to himself, what a beautiful thing as he again, once more, fixated his eyes on Monsignor's hands just like he was standing near him at Mass years ago.

They sat there, both of them, making idle chit-chat. Monsignor Kealy asked about his old parishioners, about Father Ignacio's family and the Roman political Vatican news. Sitting, talking and visiting Monsignor Kealy was a breath of fresh air for Father Ignacio and before they had even finished their lunch Father Ignacio's worries and concerns seemed to have drifted away. They talked and laughed and reminisced about the good old days when they worked together at the parish of St. Augustines'. Even though they both had a great time remembering, they both felt sad how many years had gone by. Their relationship stayed the same, but in retrospect, it did not. Father Ignacio grew up and Monsignor Kealy grew older; and life went on.

They finished their lunch and pushed their chairs away from the table. Monsignor Kealy wiped his hands with the paper knapkin supplied. *"Thank you Lord for that delicious food"* he says, and Father Ignacio follows with, *"Gracias a Dios."* (thanks be to God).

-- Best burger this side of heaven, Monsignor Kealy said.

-- I have to agree with you Monsignor, Father Ignacio replied.

-- Well Nacho, if you excuse me, I will get us some more drink.

Monsignor Kealy rose from his chair with a little more spring than he had before and walked into his house with drinking glasses in hand. Father Ignacio stood up from his chair and walked over to the porch railing as he reached into his coat pocket and pulled out a cigarette. He heard Monsignor Kealy come back out but continued to stare out into the evergreen woods ahead of him. He noticied the trees rise into the sky and touch the clouds. He took a puff from his cigarette and as he was turning around he spoke to Monsignor Kealy.

-- Monsignor, I do have to talk to you about......

Father Ignacio's voice broke short as he noticied that Monsignor wasn't there. Father Ignacio had a look of confusion on his face as he was certain that he heard Monsignor Kealy walk back out. Father Ignacio sat back down as he looked at the things on the little table next to Monsignor's rocking chair. His pipe and lighter were there and the Roman Book of Rites sat as they were before. Father Ignacio looked away back out into woods and a thought came over him as he looked back at the table and took a second look. The book underneath the Roman Book of Rites was no longer there. The book whose binder looked familar to Father Ignacio but unable to see the front cover, was mysteriously gone. Father Ignacio reached over to move the Book of Rites, when Monsignor Kealy walked out. Father Ignacio quickly sat back into his chair and puffed on his cigarette.

-- And where is the other part of my treats?, Monsignor Kealy asked.

-- I have it here of course Monsignor, Father Ignacio said as he reached in and pulled out the bag of tobacco.

-- You're my boy, Nachito, you're my boy, Monsignor said smiling as he picked up his pipe from the table.

-- Now if anybody questions, I didn't bring that to you, Father Ignacio jokingly said.

They both laughed and Monsignor Kealy tapped out his pipe on the edge of the nearby ashtray. He loaded his pipe with the new tobacco and lit it.

-- Nacho, come take a walk with me, Monsignor asked.

Monsignor Kealy tightened up his sweater as they both slowly walked down the crickety steps of the porch. Father Ignacio stuck his hands into his pockets of his long, black coat as they walked. They entered the wooded area of the seven acres that were on this property and upon entering, a cool breeze whistled through the trees as the sweet smell of nature embodied their senses. Here Monsignor Kealy asked,

-- So what cross are you carrying that has you burdened Nacho?

Monsignor Kealy has always said so much in the smallest things he says. He was definitely right. This was a cross that Father Ignacio was carrying. Everyone carries a cross that burdens one soul. It is part of being a Christian, Father Ignacio thought; and this was his cross.

Father Ignacio talked with Monsignor Kealy. The only person he felt that he can talk to frankly. He told him about meeting Makaila, about her untold story, the hidden and unspoken fear that Makaila carried and the unsurpassed secret he felt she would experience. They walked to a clearing in what seemed to be in the middle of the woods. The birds chirped above, leaves rustled underneath them and the air was clean and crisp. Moisture was in the air and the trees played their concerto with every movement of their branches and God's color canvas was all around them. This was Father Ignacio's favorite spot. Out in this clearing, two chairs overlooked the tranquil creek that flowed below them. They sat. Father Ignacio crossed his legs and draped his long coat over his lap and legs. Monsignor Kealy lit up his pipe once more and the sweet aroma of his pipe tobacco blended with the natural fragrance around them. Monsignor sighed as he began to speak

-- Well Nacho, I knew this day would come. It comes in every new priest's life, Monsignor said.

-- What do you mean Monsignor?

-- It's your ultimate test in faith my boy, Monsignor added.

Father Ignacio breathed heavily. His defenses were rising and he didn't like the feeling. "Faith? I have plenty of faith," he thought to himself. Before he could open his mouth to justify his thought, Monsignor continued speaking.

-- Not that kind of faith Nacho. This is a different kind of faith. A faith you will need to have on another fellow human being. The kind of faith you will need in yourself. This kind of faith doesn't come because you are a priest. It comes because you are a child of God.

Father Ignacio hung his head. His defenses now shattered. He knew what Monsignor was trying to tell him.

-- You will need to have faith in this Makaila person, This woman, has to have faith in herself.... and Nacho, you will need faith in yourself and in your role in this. This is the only way. Do you understand, Monsignor Kealy asked.

-- I believe I understand Monsignor. You are saying that I should not have conflict in my role in Makaila's life. I have felt that I wasn't worthy or righteous enough in trying to help Makaila.... And you are right Monsignor, Makaila feels the same way. She has felt guilt in getting me involved, wishes she never had told me. She feels so bad about anyone in her life and afraid on how it would effect them.

-- Faith, Nacho... that's all it is. Faith that your are the person God has created; with all assets and faults. Worthy enough to do God's work... righteous enough to be an instrument of God's peace.

And this is how Monsignor Kealy ended his sermon that day in the middle of the woods. Father Ignacio, cast his eyes away from Monsignor Kealy as a tear rolled down his cheek. His eyes caught a glimpse of a sunray that illuminated a stream of brilliance down in between the trees and onto the creek. Father Ignacio understood.

The walk back to the house was a silent one. The heaviness Father Ignacio felt when he first pulled up had lifted. His inner strength regained and his faith in himself restored. They had a cup of coffee together and some dessert before Father Ignacio needed to head back to the parish. Saying good-bye to Monsignor Kealy was never easy, so they always left with Monsignor making the sign of the cross upon Father Ignacio's head and making promises to meet up again and sooner next time. Father Ignacio walked to the porch steps and down to his car. Monsignor Kealy followed only up to the steps. He stopped Father Ignacio before he was able to reach his car.

-- Father Ignacio....... Monsignor said with a raised voice.

Father Ignacio stopped cold in his tracks. Monsignor Kealy had only once before called him Father Ignacio and that was at his ordination ten years ago.

-- Yes, Monsignor, Father Ignacio said with a lump in his throat.

-- You have been called. You've been chosen. This is part of your destiny in life.... life as a priest and life as a Christian. You will be very important here. God has some great plans for you. You will change something.. I know it. I have always known it.

Monsignor Kealy said these words with a raised head and pride and conviction in his voice. Father Ignacio smiled at him, raised his hand in a wave and said, "*God Bless, Monsignor*" and with that Father Ignacio stepped into his car and drove off.

Chapter Five

The Second Meeting

Sister Angelica was busy cleaning the prayer Chapel out in the garden of the rectory of St. Augustines'. Father Ignacio mentioned to her that Makaila was coming over and to clear his schedule for the rest of the afternoon. Father Ignacio was sitting in his office doing some paper work as he thought about his meeting with Makaila. His mind was cluttered with their first meeting and the words of wisdom from Monsignor Kealy. It was Father Ignacio's hope that he could learn more about the story, in hopes that Makaila would be strong enough to continue where she had left off. Father Ignacio also wanted to make certain that the last words he said to her that afternoon at the coffee house would make a little more sense to him. *"God is preparing you for something."* The only thing Father Ignacio knew was that it was not a good thing; but he did have faith in himself, he had faith in Makaila and the utmost faith in victory.

Father Ignacio leaned back in his swivel chair and lit up a cigarette. He rested his feet on the corner of his desk and gazed out the window. Children passed by on their bicycles as other children were chasing them in a playing frenzy. Father Ignacio smiled as memories of his siblings flashed through his mind. He closed his eyes for a minute in prayer. The light sound of a radio played in the background. His desk was cluttered with the typical clutter that makes its way there and stays for awhile. Magazines, last weeks newspapers, and copies of outdated church bulletins, stretched out on his desk. On the walls, a picture of the Sacred Heart of Jesus, of Pope John Paul II and a statue of the Blessed Mother "shrined" the corner of his office. On the floor were boxes of missalettes and boxes of candles and boxes of boxes. As much as Sister Angelica itched to clean up his office, Father Ignacio made her promise that she wouldn't. Sister Angelica always teased Father Ignacio by saying that one day he would get lost in his own office and that it would take a search party of twenty parishioners to dig him out.

Father Ignacio opened his eyes and noticed his cigarette had burned almost all the way down and the ashes had fallen off onto his black pants. He quickly brushed off the ashes and snuffed out the cigarette in the ashtray. Father Ignacio rose to his feet and walked through his office, through the rectory and out to the garden. Out in the chapel the sweet sound of "On Eagles' Wings", echoed throughout the garden. Sister Angelica was singing like there was no tomorrow and Father Ignacio was certain that the choirs of angels were joining her in her hymn of praise. Father Ignacio walked into the chapel especially designed for the rectory by a generous parishioner as a donation. It was a modern chapel with stained glass windows of Christ and saints, with white stucco walls and a couple of pews. In the center back wall, a wooden crucifix, another donation by a parishioner, hung. In the corner was a candle encased in a red stained glass container. The glow the candle made against the back wall and the colors that spewed from the sun through the stained glass windows gave the chapel an ambience of peace. Several times, both Sister Angelica and Father Ignacio, held private ceremonies, rosaries, vigils and prayer meetings in this chapel.... and here today, Father Ignacio and Makaila would continue on their road to whatever unfolds before them.

~ ~ ~

Makaila arrived shortly after three o'clock that afternoon. Sister Angelica made her as comfortable as she could while she waited for Father Ignacio who was next door at the church facilitating afternoon confessions. Makaila sat in the lobby of the rectory office. She fumbled for something in her purse when Father Ignacio walked in.

-- Makaila. How are you?

Makaila smiled as she closed up her purse and stood up to greet Father Ignacio. Father Ignacio held out his hand and Makaila hers and they shook hands.

-- I am fine Father, How are you? Makaila answered and asked.

-- I am well. I apologize if I kept you waiting, Father Ignacio said.

-- No, no I am fine. I just got here a couple of minutes ago myself.

Sister Angelica walks in.

-- Have you met Sister Angelica? Father Ignacio asked Makaila.

-- Not officially Father, no, Makaila answered.

-- Sister Angelica this is Makaila, Makaila... Sister Angelica, Father Ignacio said as he introduced them.

Makaila held out her hand. Sister Angelica smiled and ignored her hand and walked up and gave her a hug.

-- I don't do handshakes. They're so proper, feels like I'm making a deal, Sister Angelica said.

Makaila stretched her lips and her eyes widened as she quite didn't know what to do with Sister Angelica hugging her. She felt a bit uncomfortable but at the same time felt a strong sense of God's presence.

-- Oh, okay. Nice to meet you Sister, Makaila answered in bewilderment.

-- Good to meet you to child. Very good to meet you, Sister Angelica said as she continued to say, "Come, I need a cup of coffee, please join us."

Sister Angelica walked off as if they were supposed to follow her. Father Ignacio and Makaila smiled at each other and Father Ignacio motioned with his hand for Makaila to go on first. Makaila followed Sister Angelica behind the counter that separated the offices and the lobby and walked down a hallway that went behind the offices into another building and into the rectory kitchen. Sister Angelica walked straight to the kitchen counter, reached above her and pulled out three coffee cups and saucers.

-- Sit, sit..... Sister Angelica insisted.

-- Yes, Makaila, please have a seat, Father Ignacio agreed.

-- Thank you, Makaila said as she pulled out a chair and sat down.

Makaila looked out the window where a parfait table with four chairs were situated. Out the window Makaila noticed the tiny garden that looked very well kept and cultivated. She looked back into the kitchen as Sister Angelica was pushing Father Ignacio away as he was trying to help her with the coffee.

-- Now, now, you go sit, I'll take care of it, Sister Angelica said to Father Ignacio.

Father Ignacio smirked as he walked over to join Makaila at the table. Sister Angelica followed closely behind with sugar and cream cruets designed with green vines and pale red roses. She rushed back to the counter and retrieved two of the coffee cups and saucers and quickly returned to place them in front of Makaila and Father Ignacio.

-- You just have to learn to stay out of her way, Father Ignacio whispered to Makaila but loud enough for Sister Angelica to hear.

Makaila just smiled.

-- I heard that Father Ignacio! Sister Angelica said with a teasing tone to her voice. "Just hush," she added.

Father Ignacio and Makaila just smiled at each other. Sister Angelica came back with a pot of hot coffee and poured out the two cups. She returned to the counter and came back with her cup and she sat down and joined them. Here Sister Angelica was relentless.

-- Where are you from Makaila? Sister Angelica queried. Any brothers or sisters? Are your parents still with us?" She continued without stopping.

-- Yes, um, well, yes, I have a twin sister named Maggie. My parents are in California, there's where I grew up, Makaila answered.

Father Ignacio just smiled while he peeked over his coffee cup when Makaila looked at him.

-- Are you Catholic, Makaila? Where do you go to church? You're not a member of our parish. What parish do you belong to? Sister Angelica interrogated without blinking.

-- Sister Angelica! Please, that's more than enough questions, Father Ignacio pressed embarrassed.

-- Father, it's quite all right. Really. I don't mind, Makaila said smiling.

-- Okay, don't say I didn't warn you, Father Ignacio teased.

Sister Angelica teasingly swatted at Father Ignacio.

-- Well Sister, I grew up Protestant. My twin sister is Catholic and I have always gone to church with her in my adult years. I like the Catholic church. I have often thought of converting.

-- Well then, maybe we will see you at Sunday mass, Sister Angelica inquired.

And just like that, Sister Angelica got up from her seat, put her coffee cup down in the sink and walked off. Father Ignacio watched as she walked away without saying a good-bye.

-- That's Sister for you... She drops a bombshell and then disappears, Father Ignacio said to Makaila.

Makaila again just smiled.

-- Would you like some more coffee Makaila? Father Ignacio asked.

-- Maybe one more cup Father, thank you, Makaila said.

Father Ignacio got up from his chair and picked up the coffee pot and poured Makaila another cup as well as for himself. He sat back down and took a sip of his coffee. *"So tell me about your sister,"* he said.

Makaila was stirring her coffee. She inched up closer to the table as she lightly clinked her spoon on the edge of her cup rim and laid it gently down on her saucer.

-- Well, my twin sister and I are very close, after all, we did share a womb together. Her name is Maggie. Makaila answered. " We don't know where would be without each other."

-- Is she experiencing the same feelings you are having? Father Ignacio said so elusively.

Makaila was taken back a bit when Father Ignacio asked her this question. She saw the transformation that Father Ignacio had just made. He had gone from a relaxed person having coffee to switching hats as a person determined to get to the bottom of something.

-- Father I don't know. We both have the conscious memories of our childhood and when it all changed, but is she feeling like there's more? I believe she feels that as well, we just haven't talked about it to each other, Makaila answered.

-- Are you identical twins?, Father Ignacio asked.

-- Yes, Father, we are, Makaila responded.

-- Interesting, Father Ignacio said.

-- We can tell you lots of twin stories, Makaila said smiling.

Father Ignacio knew by her smile that she wasn't talking about the story yet unremembered, but that of their innocence, their flare for life, being mischievous and sneaky, the more normal personalities of that of being twins.

-- What does Maggie remember from your childhood?, Father Ignacio asked.

Makaila sat back into her chair as she knew that they had begun their quest. Father Ignacio's composure changed from that of a few minutes ago. He took on a more determined look, a look of "ready to do business."

-- Well, we both don't remember when they started cutting off our braids, Makaila answered..... we remember the Browns. We both remember them as not being safe people, and we both remember that life as we knew it up to that point in our lives had changed, Makaila said with choked words.

-- Is this hard for you to remember all this, Father Ignacio asked her.

58

-- It's..... it's.... just that I am so sad for the little innocent twin girls at that time. I am so sad about that, for myself and for Maggie, Makaila said with tears streaming down her cheeks.

Father Ignacio stood up and walked over to the kitchen counter where a box of Kleenix was visible. He brought the box over to Makaila, who pulled out a sheet and commenced in drying her eyes. Father Ignacio's heart opened up and he felt the blood drain out...... And he had not yet heard the details of their conscious memories.

-- Come Makaila, I have a much better place for us to talk.

Makaila followed Father Ignacio out onto the small garden through the back door of the kitchen. Makaila instantly felt the peace that enveloped her spirit. Makaila liked the feeling. It was a feeling she has felt many times whenever she was touched by God. She followed Father Ignacio into a small building and immediately she felt at ease when she walked into the chapel. Makaila sat at the front pew as Father Ignacio sat on the step in front of the small altar facing Makaila. Makaila saw the man sitting there. His heart open, his mind open and his soul open to comfort. Makaila questioned Father Ignacio's help. Why she felt she didn't deserve it, why she felt that no one could help, why she felt guilty for this one man's outstretched hand in aid, were the questions that raced through her head. As much as Makaila hated to bring this man into her life with all the daft details, she felt his comfort, his compassion and something she rarely experienced, his unconditional support and care... and Makaila felt safe inside.

-- Does your sister live near you? Father Ignacio asked.

-- Oh no, I wish she did. She lives too far away. She wishes I lived near her as well, Makaila said.

-- Do you both visit each other much? Father Ignacio continued in asking.

-- We try not to go too long without seeing each other, but we talk daily on the phone, Makaila said with a "I miss you Maggie" look on her face.

-- You miss her don't you, Makaila, Father asked as he notices Makaila's homesick face.

-- I do miss her, I miss her when we are apart too long, Makaila said with tear-filled eyes.

-- I bet, since you've shared your creation for nine months in the womb together, that it would be difficult to be away from each other too long, Father Ignacio said, trying to comfort Makaila.

Makaila reached into her hand and pulled out the ball of Kleenix she had been clutching since the questions began. Father Ignacio felt her pain as genuine as could be and Makaila felt that. Makaila grew strong momentarily.

-- And that's why we hated it when people tried to separate us, Makaila said almost angrily.

Father Ignacio just sat there, listening to every word, every letter, every pronunciation, every body language that escaped Makaila's mouth, eyes and mind. Makaila shifted in her seat.

-- Who tried to separate you two? How did they try to do that? Father Ignacio curiously asked.

-- Everyone we loved and everyone we felt unsafe about. Our parents, our school, our teachers and especially the Browns, Makaila retorted, her eyes fixed somewhere in the past.

-- Who are the Browns, Makaila?, Father Ignacio carefully asked.

-- Unsafe people, Father, unsafe and very evil people. Makaila said mechanically.

Father Ignacio saw that Makaila was somewhere else. Her eyes were not shifting, her body did not move, her breathing was a little more shallow. Makaila stared out into nowhere. Father Ignacio rose to his feet and kneeled in front of Makaila. There he gripped Makaila's hand.

-- Do you see them Makaila, do you see the Browns? Father Ignacio pressed her.

-- I see the Brown's house, Father. I see Mr. Brown and Mrs. Brown and then there's Bonnie Brown, Makaila said almost trancelike and she squeezed Father Ignacio's hand.

-- Makaila, who is the most unsafe person from those three people, Father Ignacio continued to ask.

Makaila looked down at Father Ignacio and she quickly pulled her hand away.

-- They're all evil, they're all unsafe, Makaila almost shouted.

-- It's all right Makaila, you're safe, Father Ignacio sympathetically said.

-- I am so sorry Father, I am so sorry. I didn't mean to pull away like that, Makaila said apologetically.

-- It's quite all right, Makaila. It's fine, Father Ignacio said stressing that it was really all right.

Father Ignacio reached into his coat pocket and handed Makaila a clean handkerchief.

-- Do you think you can answer my question now?, Father Ignacio asked Makaila.

Makaila straightened up, her hands wringed together, her heart skipped a beat or two, as she tried to answer Father Ignacio's question. She opened her mouth, but no words escaped.

-- It's okay, Makaila, you don't have to answer, Father Ignacio immediately said.

-- Mr. and Mrs. Brown, especially Mrs. Brown..... Makaila finally said, and Bonnie, Bonnie was evil and unsafe too.

-- Bonnie is their daughter?, Father Ignacio questioned.

-- Yes..........., Makaila said.

-- How old is she? Father Ignacio asked.

-- She was and is the same age as we are now, Makaila said, almost frightened. Father Ignacio reached up and held Makaila's hand again. Makaila responded by placing her other hand on top of Father Ignacio's hand and smiled.

-- When did you first meet Bonnie and her parents? Father Ignacio asked.

-- We met the Browns when we were in Kindergarten, Makaila answered a little more composed.

-- Did you feel unsafe then? Father Ignacio asked.

-- We did Father, both Maggie and I.......and we both felt that they were evil people even at that age, Makaila responded.

-- You said earlier, that people tried to separate both you and Maggie. Do you have any idea why they would want to do that? Father Ignacio asked her.

-- I don't know Father, Makaila hesitantly said.

-- You know Makaila, God sometimes does say that "enough is enough" and taht we don't have to know evrything, that's why His hands are much bigger than ours, Father Ignacio said.

Makaila smiled. Father Ignacio rose to his feet and sat next to Makaila on the pew. He sat there in silence for a few seconds. Father Ignacio wanted to ask so many more questions, he wanted to know so much more, instead he looked at his watch and spoke to Makaila.

-- Now, Makaila, Sister Angelica is going to invite you for dinner and I would be honored if you would join us..... and you would be doing me a favor. Sister would get after me for not insisting that you stay and have dinner with us.... so, would you stay for dinner? Father said smiling.

-- I would love to, Father, thank you, Makaila said smiling as she laughed a lighthearted laugh.

-- Very well then, Father Ignacio replied.

Father Ignacio got serious again and turned slightly to face Makaila. He spoke to her gently, sweetly and nurturing. Makaila had grown to long for that in someone, anyone.

-- I know what we just discussed must of have been very trying for you Makaila. Thank you for trusting in me, Father Ignacio said to her.

-- Father, thank you, Makaila said, with her eyes full of God's peace. Thank you for being my friend, she added.

-- Kneel with me Makaila, let us pray, Father Ignacio said to her.

Makaila watched as Father Ignacio knelt in prayer, like she was certain he has done a million times in his life. But at this particular moment, she felt like the most luckiest, most loved, most cared about, most safe person in the world. She knelt beside Father Ignacio, honored that she was asked to kneel in prayer with him. She brought her hands together and she prayed, but mainly she thanked God for creating such a wonderful instrument of His love through Father Ignacio.

As Father Ignacio knelt in prayer, he thanked God for His many blessings but mainly thanked Him for bringing a very spiritual soul into his life. He felt that he had been chosen to bring the greatness of God to being, to bring home a lost sheep back to the fold and Father Ignacio was certain it wasn't Makaila. During his prayer, Father Ignacio thought of what had transpired today in this chapel. The words and actions Makaila presented had quenched his curiosity for the moment, but God has shown Father Ignacio that his work was far from over..... but Makaila felt as though a lock had been broken, she felt lighter and her heart a little fuller. She felt completely in God's hands and nothing was ever going to remove her from there again.

Chapter Six

The Second Meeting Continues

Father Ignacio and Makaila retired into the living room of the rectory. Sister Angelica stayed behind as she insisted that she clean up after dinner.

-- I'll bring in some coffee in a minute, Sister Angelica yelled from behind the kitchen wall.

Father Ignacio sat in his wing back chair and Makaila sat on the couch facing Father Ignacio. They waited for their coffee Sister Angelica promised. A few seconds later Sister Angelica came into the living room with a tray of coffee and some pound cake.

-- Oh, Sister, you shouldn't have gone to all that trouble, Makaila insisted.

-- No trouble at all my dear, Sister Angelica responded.

She set the tray down on the coffee table.

-- Well, I'm going to skip on coffee and dessert this evening. I am running late for a meeting at the church. Is there anything else I can get for you Father before I leave? Sister Angelica asked.

-- No, no.. you run along. We'll be fine, Father Ignacio replied, "and thank you Sister," he added.

Sister Angelica picked up a glass that was sitting on the mantle and returned to the kitchen. A few seconds later, the back door to the kitchen opened and closed. Father Ignacio lit up a cigarette and Makaila sipped her coffee.

-- I want to talk to you about when you and Maggie were seven, Father Ignacio asked Makaila.

Makaila shifted in her seat again. She sat her coffee down on the wooden table that separated Father Ignacio and herself. She leaned back into the couch as her hands straightened out her skirt.

-- Okay Father, she said almost cowardly.

-- Is that the year they cut off your braids? Father Ignacio questioned.

The air around the living room seemed to have grown tense when Father Ignacio asked this question. The tension that Makaila emitted was strong enough for Father Ignacio to feel. He knew that the circumstance surrounding the incident when their braids were cut was a significant part to their story. He just didn't know what that would entail.

~ ~ ~

Makaila and Maggie were six years old when things in their home were beginning to change. Their mother grew quieter and her temper shorter. She started going out at night with people from the neighborhood. Makaila admired her mothers' beauty whenever she got dressed up to go out. Makaila and Maggie noticed that extra "glee" in her step when she went out for dancing lessons, but they weren't certain that's really where their mother was going. Things at home were indeed changing. The subtle control that the twins experienced on a daily basis was too subtle to have been noticed by anyone outside the immediate family; but it was there. The only one who ever seemed to have noticed and always looked like she wanted to say something was their grandmother. Grandma Bella was Lalee's mother; and the twins' saving grace when things at home got too bad. Makaila always felt that Grandma Bella knew much more than she let on, and Makaila also always felt that Grandma Bella wanted to say something that had her mind occupied; some secret, some lie, something that was not right and she always walked around knowing this and always bit her tongue when she, on occasion, said too much. But Grandma Bella never said enough to put pieces together. Makaila has memories of when Lalee and Grandma Bella would be on the telephone arguing about something that Lalee shouldn't be doing. The relationship between Lalee and Bella was not any better from that when Lalee was a teenager. Lalee always voiced that she hated her mother and Grandma Bella always fought for Lalee's' love. The twins always enjoyed going over to Grandma Bella's house. They played house together and had tea parties, but to Makaila, Grandma Bella always had some mystery about her, but the sad thing about this was that the mystery was not about herself, it was concerning her daughter Lalee. Grandma Bella always talked to the twins in a way that made them feel to be on the look out, to protect themselves and to trust what they sense and see. Makaila always questioned Grandma Bella's words, but Grandma out of respect, or maybe out of fear, always said not so much. One particular day, while Grandma Bella and Makaila were in the upstairs bedroom of her home, Grandma Bella gazed out the window.

-- Something strange happens in that backyard, Grandma Bella said in a voice that whispered cold in the room.

-- Where Grandma? Makaila asked.

Grandma Bella, slowly turned from the window and onto Makaila's face. She looked down as if staring at an angel. She grabbed Makaila's face with both her hands... she smiled.

-- Nothing darling, nothing at all, Grandma Bella said. "But you must promise me something," she continued.

Makaila jumped on her lap and looked her in the eye.

-- What Grandma Bella? Makaila questioned.

-- You must promise me that you will always protect yourself; you and Maggie, take care of each other, will you promise me that? Grandma Bella asked Makaila.

-- We will Grandma Bella, we promise, Makaila joyfully said as she put her arms around her grandmother's neck.

-- Well, darling, let's go downstairs for some cookies and milk huh?, Grandma Bella said.

Makaila jumped off Grandma Bella's lap and watched her grandmother slowly rise from her chair. She looked at her grandmother's face that had a happy look about it, but sad and somber eyes. Makaila always questioned why her mother

Lalee did not like her own mother and why they always fought. Makaila always questioned the things Lalee would say about Grandma Bella. Makaila couldn't find it her heart to believe the bad things Lalee said about Grandma Bella.

Makaila remembers the stories that Lalee used to say about her grandmother. Lalee and Jack always said that Grandma Bella is a liar and a manipulator and voiced out that they did not like her much. Makaila just felt that something was not right. Someone was not telling the truth and someone was holding in the truth, but Makaila was unclear as to which one.

-- Makaila sweetheart, are you coming down?, Grandma Bella shouted from the kitchen below.

-- Coming Grandma Bella, Makaila shouted back.

Makaila stood up to walk downstairs, she looked out the window. She questioned Grandma Bella's statement, *"Something strange happens in that backyard."* Makaila felt a chill that climbed up her spine and felt uneased. She did not like this feeling and she quickly turned, walked away and ran downstairs. But Grandma Bella was her safe place, her safe person and Makaila and Maggie could sit on her lap forever. Regardless on how their parents felt about Grandma Bella, that didn't stop the twins from loving her as much as they did; and their parents felt this insane jealousy about that.

~ ~ ~

Back at the twins' house things were almost normal; normal enough not to raise any suspicions anyway. Lalee was spending a lot more time away from home at night and her drinking had gotten worse. She was spending time with the Browns and the other neighbors and Lalee's attitude about the twins was changing. She no longer played house with them, or made dress clothes for their dolls, but Makaila and Maggie still longed to be close to her. To them, this was their mother and they couldn't imagine that things could get any worse than they were. But it did.

Makaila and Maggie started kindergarten and their family started having the Browns in their lives. Makaila met Bonnie in the same grade and what Makaila thought was a best friend turned out to be her worst nightmare. Bonnie was a homely looking girl, she had long black hair and eyes as dark as coal. Her body was tanned and her legs long and slender. Makaila was forced to invite Bonnie over to her house because Lalee felt sorry for her because she was an only child. As much as Makaila tried to stay away from Bonnie, the more Bonnie was in her life.... and the worst Bonnie was with Makaila. The nightmares really started when Makaila started to spend the night at the Browns house.

~ ~ ~

Father Ignacio looked at Makaila as she was telling this part of her story. Makaila was in a far off land, and certainly was not in the rectory of St. Augustine's. Father Ignacio saw the anger and the frustration on Makaila's face and Father Ignacio knew for certain that Makaila's true emotions were being released.

-- Makaila, did you ever find out what your grandmother was talking about? Father Ignacio asked her.

Makaila did not move nor did she answer.

-- Makaila? Makaila? Father Ignacio tried to get her attention. Without skipping a beat, Makaila answered.

-- About what Father, she asked.

-- About the strange things happening at the neighbor's?, Father Ignacio continued. "Did you ever find out what she was talking about?"

Makaila looked disturbed at Father Ignacio's question. Makaila was momentarily confused and looked like she did not know what Father Ignacio was talking about. Finally, Makaila cleared her throat and her eyes returned back from the glossy stare she had.

-- No, Father, we never did find out from Grandma what she knew about it, Makaila finally answered.

-- Do you know what was going on over there? Father Ignacio asked.

-- Not at that house, but at the Brown's house I knew what was happening there and I could only bet that it was the same at both those houses.

-- What was happening there, Makaila? Father Ignacio asked.

-- Something hateful, something not good, something that I always felt danger about. Something I could never see but only felt, Makaila said almost slipping into the couch.

-- What did you feel exactly? Father Ignacio pressed her.

-- I felt darkness, Makaila said. "I felt darkness" as these word traced off her lips softly.

Makaila closed her eyes and lifted her hands up to her face to cover them. Father Ignacio felt her fear and her pain and felt her confusion.

-- I also knew that they wanted to hurt us, they hated us; all of them, Makaila retorted back at Father Ignacio.

-- Who? Father Ignacio asked.

-- Mom and Dad, Mr. & Mrs. Brown, Bonnie, they all hated us; and they wanted us out of the picture, Makaila said, holding back tears.

-- How do you think your parents hated you? Father Ignacio asked.

-- I was confused at my parents for treating us badly, Makaila said in a raised tone.

-- And that's what you makes you think that they hated you two? Father Ignacio asked, knowing that Makaila would react to this question.

-- NO!, there's more... They did lots of mean things to us as parents. Cruel things, hateful things. They said and did things to us, Makaila shouted.

-- Said things? What kind of things? Father Ignacio questioned.

Makaila's eyes filled with more tears than ever, tears rolled down her cheek. Makaila looked down at her feet and slowly raised her head.

-- Our mother said to me one day, Makaila barely getting the words out her mouth. "She said, she said," Makaila tried saying the words though she was choking on her own tears, "she said, I tried getting rid of you as kids...."

Makaila sunk into her body as her head leaned forward. Sobs of painful cries echoed throughout the living room of the rectory. Makaila's body shook with such force, tears dropped to the carpet below. Makaila's cries of hurt and pain fell to the floor with the teardrops. Father Ignacio was also taken back with the words he heard that came out of Makaila's voice. He rose from his chair and walked over to Makaila. He couldn't imagine the hurtful pain that she felt. What kind of mother tells something like that to her child? Father Ignacio felt every painful tear that fell from her face and he wanted desperately to make it better. He sat next to Makaila and held onto her shoulders. Makaila cried so deeply that the tension in the room echoed off the walls. Father Ignacio could not say a word. What could he say? What could he possibly say that her spirit already doesn't know? Father Ignacio's spirit went out to her and Father Ignacio then realized that a tear was rolling down his own cheek. He knelt in front of her and placed his hands in the top of Makaila's head and silently offered a prayer of peace, the hurt to go away and of strength. Makaila slowly regained control. Her painful sobs reverted to hurtful tears. Father Ignacio wiped away his tear by the time Makaila looked up at him. The tension that surrounded Makaila had dissipated, a calm peace enveloped her, she glowed as Father Ignacio released his hands over Makaila's head. Makaila grabbed both of Father Ignacio's hands into her own as he was bringing down his action of healing and blessing. She held tight onto Father Ignacio's hands. Father

Ignacio smiled as Makaila smiled as she was saying, "thank you."

-- Are you all right now, Makaila? Father Ignacio said.

Makaila answered that she was fine and also noticed for the first time the Spanish accent Father Ignacio possessed in his voice.

-- Would you like some more coffee? Father Ignacio asked Makaila while rising to his feet. "or maybe a glass of wine at this point," Father Ignacio half teased.

-- A glass of wine sounds good right about this time, Makaila answered with a smile to her face, knowing that they both were leading that way to begin with.

-- A glass of wine it is then, Father Ignacio said as he walked over to the cart that sat next to the bookshelf to the right of his chair.

Father Ignacio walked across the room and poured out two wine glasses. As he was walking back to the center of the room, Sister Angelica walked in.

-- Whew, what a walk and what a meeting!, Sister Angelica said. What have you two been doing all this time? she added.

Sister Angelica looked at Makaila while she said this and noticed that Makaila had been crying. She quickly changed the subject to Father Ignacio who was standing there with the two wine glasses.

-- Wine? You were going to invite me weren't you? Sister Angelica asked.

-- Yes of course, Sister, Father Ignacio said. Here take mine, Father Ignacio offered.

-- I can get my own thank you, Sister Angelica said stoutly.

-- Let me help you, Father Ignacio said as he quickly took the other wine glass to Makaila and joined Sister Angelica at the cart.

-- Father are you all right?, Sister Angelica whispered to Father Ignacio. You look perplexed, she continued.

-- Yes Sister, I'm fine, Father Ignacio replied.

Sister Angelica poured out the wine into the glass that Father Ignacio was holding for her. Her eyes met his as if saying, "you're not all right," Father Ignacio could only smile. Sister Angelica set the bottle of wine back on the cart while Father Ignacio put the cork back in. Sister took a sip of her glass while she looked at the paneled wall in front of her as she turned around to face Makaila. Father Ignacio was setting everything back on the cart as if he was killing time. Father Ignacio was just trying to compose himself as well. His back was towards Makaila and it was Sister Angelica who now was speaking to Makaila.

-- Lord, what a meeting. I almost had to pull out the Holy Water on some of those people. You would think I was at the Youth Group meeting.

-- What kind of meeting was it Sister? Makaila asked.

-- Well, believe it or not, it was the Women's Altar Society, Sister Angelica said cracking a laugh.

Makaila smiled and laughed with her. Father Ignacio finally turned around and faced Sister Angelica and Makaila.

-- I am confident you took care of them, Father Ignacio asked Sister Angelica.

-- With the grace of God, yes, Sister Angelica answered. "Well, I should get out of your way and retire to the offices; and let you continue to whatever you were doing," she added.

Father Ignacio sat back down into his chair.

-- No, please stay and at least finish your drink with us, Makaila asked.

Sister looked at Makaila and at Father Ignacio who smiled at her.

-- Well okay, thank you my dear, I think I will, Sister Angelica said surprisingly. "You know, it's not very often that Father Ignacio lets me out of my room," she jokingly added.

-- Sister, don't say such things. She just might believe you! Father Ignacio joked back.

-- I find that very hard to believe. I have never met a person like Father Ignacio, Makaila sweetly said.

-- Yes, Father Ignacio is definitely very special. We all are, but Father Ignacio received special blessings at his birth and especially at his ordination. He is destined to do great things, Sister Angelica said proudly.

-- I am certain that he will, Makaila justified.

-- Yes, that's why I promised to watch over him, Sister Angelica continued.

Sister Angelica quickly took a sip of her wine, looking and feeling that she had said too much. Father Ignacio looked at Sister Angelica puzzled and looked a little confused about her last statement. Sister Angelica immediately changed the subject.

-- So my dear, what has you so upset? Sister Angelica asked Makaila.

-- Its what my mother did, Makaila said.

-- Sometimes mothers do things that they are not proud of, Sister Angelica responded.

-- Well it's much more than that, but the funny thing is, I still love her, Makaila said looking at Father Ignacio. "Despite the things she did and said", she added.

-- You have a strong spirit my child, Sister Angelica said to Makaila as she tapped on Makaila's hand.

Father Ignacio finally spoke.

-- Your soul is destined to survive Makaila. The reason you hurt so much is because you've experienced unconditional love for another person.

Both Makaila and Sister Angelica sat there in silence for a moment. Makaila's eyes once again filled with tears. This time the tears were of peace, of happiness, of clear emotion. Father Ignacio felt better. He knew for certain that Makaila would hold onto what he just said, and the peculiar thing about that was that his soul said that and not Father Ignacio. His soul felt that Makaila needed to know and believe this in herself. Father Ignacio felt that Makaila would need to hold onto this as she was destined to do something great in her life as well. Sister Angelica really didn't know what to say. She turned from Father Ignacio and looked at Makaila. She took hold of Makaila's hand in hers.

-- That's the kind of love God has for all His children, Sister Angelica said as the only thing she can think of to say.

-- Thank you Sister, Makaila said almost whisper like.

-- Amen, Father Ignacio replied.

Makaila smiled as her heart smiled. She gave thanks to God at this moment for having brought these wonderful people into her life at this particular point in her life, especially Father Ignacio. Her soul was driven to be near Father Ignacio's soul and she only felt safe for probably the first time in her life from someone apart from God. And what a wonderful feeling it was. It reminded her of being free, of being able to skip down the sidewalk. She felt at this moment the same feeling she had when she no longer had to go to the Brown's house when she was a child. She felt free then, happy, skipped all the way to school and Maggie questioned her on her absolute joy. "I feel free!" she would say to her twin sister, "I feel free!" and now her soul was saying the same thing, "I feel a little more free," it would say and Makaila could feel her soul embracing her, but at the same time she could feel Maggie's pull on her pajamas. Makaila for the first time felt that she needed to help Maggie, but Makaila couldn't do that until she was completely free and Makaila also had the strange thought that Maggie had to free herself; and behind it all, the question still lingered, "free from what...?"

At the same moment, Father Ignacio felt his spirit stir within him. Father Ignacio felt that his soul stood on guard. He felt that he was destined to free someone, to free a spirit, to free a mind, to free a thought, to free bonds that tighten, to free the innocent, to free the forgiven, but the question that pounded in his mind like a train was, "free who and free from what?"

-- Well my dears, I think it is time for me to say my nightly prayers and head off to an early sleep, Sister Angelica said as she sipped her last drink from her wine glass.

-- Good night Sister and thank you again, Makaila said as she stood to hug Sister Angelica.

-- What a good learner you are, Sister Angelica said to Makaila, noticing the hug that Makaila was offering. "Good night my dear," she tenderly said.

-- Good night Sister, I'll see you in the morning. Have a pleasant evening and a restful sleep, Father Ignacio said as he stood up.

-- And you, Sister Angelica said to Father Ignacio, "don't stay up too late, you have morning Mass tomorrow."

-- Yes Sister, Father Ignacio said with sarcasm in his voice.

-- Well, God be with you both, Sister Angelica said as she disappeared into the kitchen and down the hall to her room.

Father Ignacio settled back down into his chair and Makaila did the same. He lit up a cigarette as more work needed to be done here.

Chapter Seven

The Conscious Memories

Makaila again stood up from her chair, walked over to the coffee cart and placed her wine glass down. She looked around the living room and Father Ignacio sat contemplating his next thought. Makaila noticed the crucifix above the fireplace and the books on the book shelf. She also noticed the outdated furniture that decorated the living room and the table lamps you would buy at a yard sale years ago. In Makaila's mind it quite reminded her of her house growing up; and the feeling was disturbing but yet, a sweet homesick feeling came over her. Makaila missed what could have been and not what it became. Father Ignacio watched Makaila as she walked around the living room as if she were touring a museum and looking and admiring the artifacts. Father Ignacio puffed on his cigarette wondering and thinking if Makaila has already gone through too much tonight. Maybe he thought, he would ask her to come to the church one night this week and finish off where they left off today. He also thought of the memories that Makaila brought to his ears. Makaila remembered many things, her grandmother, the Browns, her parents, and Bonnie. But there's more, much more and Father Ignacio did not know where to go from here. It was Makaila who set the stage for the next set of stories she had to tell, stories she needed to tell, stories that should have been told years ago.

Father Ignacio watched Makaila as she paced back and forth in the room. Her strength and certain spirit allowed her to become calm and peaceful even after a traumatic experience or thought. It was this kind of certainty that Father Ignacio admired in a person. That certainty that regardless how bad things may seem, they don't last forever and the assurance that God brings better and nicer rewards. Makaila walked around the room as if waiting for an interrogation. She looked again at the bookshelf and it made her think of the disturbing dream she had about Father Ignacio. The thought of the dream alone sent her memories racing across her head. What was it about that book that stood open on the very top of a bookshelf with such great light that made Father Ignacio fall to the floor? What did the book signify? What did Father Ignacio have to do with this book anyway and why was Father Ignacio in her dream that seemed almost to close to a memory?

-- Father Ignacio, could we sit outside, Makaila asked.

-- Yes, we certainly can, Father Ignacio replied.

Outside the sun had just settled in for its nighttime rest and the moon rose slowly in the sky. Makaila walked out followed by Father Ignacio. Makaila took a deep breath and whiffed in a healthy dose of peace. Father Ignacio did the same. A breath of fresh air did them both good. It was a feeling of refreshment, a feeling of a long awaited cleansing and a feeling of clearness.

-- Its a beautiful evening Makaila, Father Ignacio said as he looked around and stared at the horizon.

-- Yes, it is very nice Father, Makaila answered.

-- Its wonderful when the seasons change. It's feeling of renewal, I believe, Father Ignacio continued.

-- Does your soul ever renew Father? Makaila asked.

-- No, but I believe that your soul renews your spirit, Father Ignacio responded.

Makaila just nodded her head in acknowledgment as she herself looked out into the now darkening sky. Father Ignacio sat at the patio table that sat in the middle of the grassy area. Makaila walked around nearby as she looked at all the plants and flowers that brought in a hypnotizing fragrance to the garden. Makaila's face was turned away from Father Ignacio when she finally spoke.

-- You know Father, I don't even remember when they first cut our braids, Makaila said quietly as if trying to remember. "It was like one day we had braids and we woke up the next morning without them," she added.

-- Why is the cutting of your braids so significant to you, Father Ignacio asked.

-- There's where everything changed for both of us, Maggie and me.

-- Changed? Like how? Father Ignacio inquired.

-- We were forbidden to have long hair ever again. As soon as our hair grew enough to put into a braid, we got haircuts.

-- Did anyone ever explain to you why your braids were cut? Father Ignacio asked.

-- No one said anything about it, except Bonnie, Makaila said.

Makaila quickly sat down in the chair opposite Father Ignacio. She placed her elbows on the table and rested her body into the chair.

-- What did Bonnie say about your haircuts? Did she tease you about it? Father Ignacio asked.

-- No she did not, Makaila answered. It was quite the opposite, she continued.

-- She liked your haircut? Father Ignacio once again questioned.

-- No, it was more like, she knew something about why our braids were cut off in the first place. She let us know that we were not allowed to have braids, Makaila said.

-- Why would Bonnie care about your hair? Father Ignacio asked.

-- Just to be mean. She knew how much Maggie and I loved our braids, and she teased us by telling us that we weren't allowed to have long hair and that we never will, Makaila replied.

Makaila's face became angry as she told her story of the anguish and torment she felt about when they cut off their braids. Makaila and Maggie were always proud of their long hair. Makaila can remember running, crying, screaming and begging their mother to not cut their hair. Their hair was cut so short it looked like a bowl was placed on their head and their hair cut around it. Makaila felt so humiliated, so sick and felt torment whenever this routine happened. Makaila can remember one day when she as nine years old walking with Bonnie, when she mentioned that she wanted to let her hair grow long and Bonnie answered that "your mother won't let you, I'm the only one who can have long hair." Makaila could not believe her ears. She was dumbfounded, "what in the world was she talking about..." she thought to herself. But Bonnie was right. At one point, her hair was long enough and one of her aunts put it in a braid for her. Makaila even thought that maybe she would be able to keep it long. She was wrong. Makaila's hair was even cut shorter. Lalee, Makaila's mother was very clever. She always made it sound that it would be easier on her if the twins had short hair and everyone believed her. Everyone wanted things to be easier for Lalee, even Makaila; and Makaila was confused about that.

-- Do you believe that cutting off your braids was something more than making it easier for your mother? Father Ignacio asked.

-- Yes, I believe it was much more. I think the Browns cut off our braids the first time. I don't remember when they were first cut. All we know is that one day we didn't have them anymore, Makaila said with tear-filled eyes.

-- And how did you feel when you first realized your braids were gone? Father Ignacio continued in asking.

-- I always felt terror, a lot of terror and complete sadness, Makaila answered.

-- Seems to me that you felt that your innocence was being stripped from you, that they were in control. Is that what it felt like? Father Ignacio asked Makaila.

-- Yes, it feels that way Father, Makaila said in a low voice.

-- And you feel the Browns have something to do with that? Father Ignacio added.

-- They have to do with a lot of changes in our lives then, especially when we had to go to their house, Makaila replied.

-- So tell me about the Brown's house and you and Maggie going over there, Father Ignacio insisted.

Makaila stood up from her chair and looked up into the heavens. She stuck her hands into her skirt pockets and sighed heavily. The sky was a little darker and the breeze a little cooler. Normal daytime sounds were barely audible while the nighttime noises began to chime in. Makaila's mind tried to escape the vivid memories from coming too fast, and short of trying, she could not. She again sighed as she sat back down and faced Father Ignacio.

Father Ignacio knew that the next few stories of her memory would be harder than the ones they just visited. Father Ignacio knew that Makaila was fighting her memories from approaching too quickly. Again Father Ignacio thought they had talked enough, but then Makaila was the one who insisted on continuing.

Father Ignacio's soul jumped within him and visions of a house and the upstairs and a backyard came to him. The only problem was he didn't know whose house it was. He shook his head as the vision disappeared from him.

Makaila didn't understand why she had to go the Brown's house so often. She really did not like Bonnie and yet Makaila felt as though she was being forced into being with her. Makaila never liked spending time alone with Bonnie, but it always seemed the grown-ups were never around and that's when Bonnie was at her meanest. Bonnie had always said things that didn't make sense, things that Makaila didn't believe anyhow. But the strange thing about it is that

Makaila always felt a subtle fear to Bonnie's threats.

Bonnie had always physically threatened Makaila when she would tackled her to the ground and tortured her by tickling her. Makaila would always scream for help but no one was ever around. Bonnie always came back with subtle, scary remarks by saying, "this is how we torture people," and "we could tickle you until you wouldn't be able to breath." Bonnie, as thin as she was, was much stronger than Makaila so getting Bonnie to get off of her was almost impossible. Makaila always felt trapped and suffocated.

Bonnie always said things just enough to raise questions but never enough to believe them. Bonnie's threats included remarks like, "you are next" and "that will happen to you." Makaila was scared every time Bonnie mentioned these things and Makaila's sense of defense was, "I don't believe you," but a part of Makaila did.

Makaila mentioned a particular day one summer, where she had to go to the country with the Browns. Makaila hated to ride in the car with the Browns because that meant that they were on their way to the country. Makaila always felt this incredible fear about going. She was confused why she had to go at all, but worse than that Makaila always sensed that she wouldn't come back from there alive anyway, and what a horrible feeling that was for a little blond haired, blue-eyed girl.

In the country was where Bonnie was her cruelest. Whenever they went to the country, Bonnie's cousin would meet them up there and she was meaner than Bonnie. She had a mean spirit. She was obese, frumpy and downright gross looking. The adults always seemed to disappear somewhere and the scary thing is you never knew where they went. One minute they were there, and the next they weren't. The children were always left to tend to themselves and Makaila hated that. That is when scary, insensible remarks were made and Bonnie's actions became stronger.

At the country there was a pond and Bonnie and her cousin would not let Makaila up to the waters edge after swimming in it. They kept taunting her and pushing her back into the muddy, dirty, and slimy water. It seemed that everything Bonnie and her cousin did was planned and short of directed. Makaila had no survival instincts and she just prayed for the moment she would get back home. With the physical threats came the subtle innuendos about something secret, something mysterious, something dark and evil.

Bonnie and her cousin made it a point to tell Makaila that they were not allowed in the barn behind the house. Makaila felt such terror, such darkness, such despair that she often wondered when she would get back home. She missed her family, especially Maggie and she couldn't get home fast enough.

-- Why do you think Bonnie was mean to you? Father Ignacio asked.

-- I don't know Father, I feel she was programmed to hate me or hate us anyway, Makaila answered.

-- Did this kind of thing only happen at the country? Father Ignacio questioned.

-- Oh no, it was even at home, especially at her house, at school, or just every time we were together, Makaila said.

-- And what sort of things happened when you were together with her? Father Ignacio asked.

-- Lots of things. She talked about ceremonies and sacrifices and that they would do that to me, Makaila answered almost scared-like.

--What did she mean by that? Father Ignacio asked her.

-- We watched a television show one time where a young girl was sacrificed and thrown into a volcano, she said that they would do that to me, Makaila answered.

Father Ignacio's curiosity got the better of him. His skin crawled with every word that Makaila said. The story started out as a mystery and the pieces were finally fitting into place. Father Ignacio knew now that the story that was going to unfold was an unholy one. But Father Ignacio had so many questions now, and he knew that Makaila really couldn't answer them... and he couldn't answer them either at this moment. Father Ignacio knew that much more needed to be said and much more needed to be revealed. Father Ignacio just didn't know how much Makaila knew or how much more was going to be revealed to her.... or to him.

-- What do you remember about the Brown's house? Father Ignacio asked Makaila.

Makaila looked as if Father Ignacio asked a loaded question. Her face reverted to a scared, terror-filled look. Father Ignacio knew that what he asked was a hard road that Makaila was going to embark on. Father Ignacio looked at

Makaila and could sense her fear and torment. He had a feeling as well and hecouldn't quite place his emotion. It was an uncomfortable feeling. It was a feeling he often did not feel. He questioned it. What was it? What was the emotion he was experiencing? He recognized his strength, he knew about the sadness he pitied for Makaila. He recounted the stories he had already heard from Makaila and he knew that it was already too much for anyone to have to have gone through.... and like a bolt of lightening and a shiver in his body, Father Ignacio recognized the emotion. The more he recognized it the clearer it got. Father Ignacio was surprised, but what he was feeling, was a feeling of anger. A feeling he never did like and a feeling he didn't want to have. Father Ignacio had a bigger question though; why was he even feeling that to begin with? He knew he had to continue with Makaila and for the first time since meeting Makaila he knew his purpose. He knew that God was using him in freeing Makaila from her memories but he wasn't totally convinced how much he was to be involved; or how much Makaila wanted or needed him to be.

Makaila sat there, contemplating the question Father Ignacio just asked her. She felt the sudden shiver rise from her stomach up to her throat. Remembering the Brown's house was as vivid as to her now as it was then. As a child, she dreaded the times she had to go there and as an adult she loathed when she had to revisit it in memory. She felt angry and confused at so many people when a visit to the Browns was talked about. She was mad at her mother Lalee, for making her go over there, she was sad at her father Jack, for not coming for her when she felt afraid and she was hurt at Bonnie for the torment Makaila felt when she was there.

-- Did you have to go often, Father Ignacio asked her.

-- It felt like I had to go over there a lot, Makaila answered.

-- And it was something you didn't want to do? Father Ignacio pressed her to answer.

-- No, I never wanted to go over there, not again, not ever, Makaila said.

-- Can you tell me what it was like at the Browns' house? Father Ignacio asked again.

Makaila shut down immediately. Father Ignacio did not know if he were to get an answer from Makaila and he wasn't sure if he wanted to hear it. The emotions that came into his heart and mind were uncomfortable for him. Was he too involved? Why this special story and why in this special part was he placed? Why is this story different from the other many stories he has heard in his role as a Catholic Church counselor? Why did he need to know more and why at the same time did he not need to hear anymore?

The sweat on Makaila's brow was beginning to show. Her body temperature seemed to have raised with every passing memory that flashed into her con-science. Her body tensed up as her shoulders disappeared into her neck. Her voice cracked a bit when she started describing the Browns' house and its occupants. Know one knew this story and it is the first time that she has spoken of it to anyone else apart from Maggie; and traveling down this path is going to be a difficult one for Makaila, one that is certainly going to be very informative to Father Ignacio.

~ ~ ~

Makaila immediately felt the fear at the Browns' house. The living room was always dark. Dark furniture embossed the room that seemed to have a certain air about it. Dark oak furniture, the shades and curtains always drawn, lamps that weren't even plugged in filled the room. It had one wall in dark paneling, while the other wall had a reddish wallpaper look to it. In the center of the room, was a round coffee table, a knick knack of some sort under a laced, dark brown doily. One wall hosted two bookshelves, one on each end of the wall with more dust than there were books. In the center, there was a desk with a single desk lamp that sort of looked like a dragon, a couple of envelopes, some paper and a pen.

In the kitchen there was always light. There was a table with four chairs and the chairs had blue vinyl backing and chrome legs. In the center of the table was a glass rooster that had some sugar in it. The stove always seemed to have some sort of pot brewing, though odor was really never noticed. The sink had dirty dishes in it and the linoleum flooring always seemed to need a good mopping. There was an off-yellow color refrigerator in the corner and it was never opened in Makaila's presence. The kitchen was always off limits and forbidden territory and Bonnie always made it a point to make certain that Makaila understood that. Makaila always asked what they were doing in there and Bonnie would always describe something sickening and scary.

~ ~ ~

Makaila jumped up from her seat and started pacing around the garden where Father Ignacio sat. Father Ignacio watched her as she changed into a panicky, frightened woman. Makaila brushed the hair from her mouth as she held onto her necklace of charms that hung around her neck. It was then that Father Ignacio noticed for the first time a couple of small crucifixes and heart-shaped charm that laced her neckline. Father Ignacio watched as she paced and looked out into the horizon as if she was lost and had no idea where to turn. Father Ignacio felt peculiar at this point as well. He thought and thought about what Makaila just described to him and his mind wandered for a minute.

-- Makaila, are you all right? Father Ignacio asked.

-- In the kitchen, Father, there was a door that led outside to the backyard and a door that led to the basement, Makaila said barely making out the words.

Makaila quickly sat down. Her body seemed to shake with every passing memory that flashed before her inner vision. Her mouth became dry and her hands became sweaty. Her heartbeats came closer and louder. The feeling in her legs was that of wanting to run, just run and not look back. It was the same feeling she has experienced in her adult life whenever she was triggered. Makaila always had this same feeling whenever she was confronted with mice, gross, bloody things and basements. She suffered from posttraumatic stress, but everyone knew it only as the "scared twins." All her friends knew it from her childhood. As Makaila grew older, the posttraumatic stress got worse and the worst was that Makaila had no idea at that time why she reacted the way she did about these certain things; and Makaila was having one of those moments.

-- Makaila, can you hear me? Father Ignacio pressed.

-- Yes Father. I'm all right, she said not quite believing it herself.

-- What were you feeling just now? Father Ignacio asked her.

-- Fear Father, fear and I have no idea why, Makaila answered.

-- What made you feel that way, I mean, what part of your thoughts frightened you? Father Ignacio asked.

-- The basement... when I started talking about the basement, that's what triggered me. I feel my body racing inside, Makaila said.

-- What is it about the basement that scares you so? Father Ignacio asked.

-- I don't know. But I do know that Bonnie always scared us about the basement.

-- How so, Father Ignacio inquired.

In the kitchen there was the door to the basement. In Makaila's memory, she often saw the door and at times she recalled that there was no door. At times they were allowed to play in the basement and Makaila always felt this coldness when they walked down there. At the beginning of the basement it looked like a normal basement where a washer and dryer were situated. It had white linoleum flooring and a chalkboard where Bonnie always drew but off to the other side it seemed like the illumination of the fluorescent lighting above ended at a certain point; and beyond that.... darkness; an area where they were forbidden to cross or play in. The Browns' house had more than one place or area that was forbidden for them to play in or be in. Bonnie instilled such fear into Makaila that it seemed that she was ordered to do so.

One particular day while both Makaila and Bonnie were skating down the street, they stopped to pet a cat who had found his way in between some parked cars. They continued to skate down the hill when they heard a braking screech sound. When they skated back up the hill they found the cat that was hit by a passing car. At dinner that afternoon at the Browns' house, Bonnie made mention of the cat with some sort of association with the basement. Mrs. Brown pinched Bonnie under the table so hard and told her never to mention that again. That conversation immediately stopped and Makaila felt petrified. Bonnie never seemed to get into any trouble, but that night she did. Bonnie hated her mother and Makaila never knew why, but Bonnie made it clear that she did.

Spending the night at the Brown's was the worse feeling Makaila felt. She just wanted to go home. She wanted to be safe and she longed for her dad to protect her. Makaila felt in her heart that her father would protect her even though Bonnie on numerous occasions would say; "don't ever tell what goes on here, no one would believe you, especially your dad. It would be worse the next time if you tell." And there was always a next time. Makaila's house was only two and half blocks away, but Makaila felt that she couldn't get to her parents. Makaila couldn't figure out why her parents didn't know what when on there. Makaila also felt that if they did, they would never let her go over to the Brown's ever again.

By night time, things got stranger and scarier at the Brown's house. Makaila always laid wide awake at night, she could feel her heart pound out of her chest. Her only comfort was that a light from a nearby street lamp shining into the room. This was the time where she begged her dad to come and get her. Her fear was more intense when Mr. Brown would come into the room with only his underwear and picked up Bonnie and take her to his bed. Makaila was so afraid he would come in the middle of the night and take her one.

~ ~ ~

-- Dad! Why didn't you come get me! Makaila shouted into the night as tears streamed down her cheeks.

Father Ignacio was startled in his chair. Makaila just stopped in her story and without warning just shouted what she probably needed to shout for many years. Father Ignacio's heart stopped and felt the anguish and pain and sadness that Makaila was now experiencing. Makaila sat in her chair and cried and between muffled sounds Father Ignacio heard her say, "I needed my dad to come and protect me. ... and he never came." as she started to calm down a bit. Her tears dropped onto the cheeks and down her chin as they landed on her lap. Tears from many years ago, tears that have welled up inside her, waiting to be drained. Her tears waited to fall probably as long as Makaila waited for her father to come get her.

-- I am so sorry Makaila, I am so sorry, Father Ignacio said with a hurting heart.

-- I never understood why they never knew what was going on over there, Makaila answered.

Makaila dried her eyes as her lungs filled-up with fresh air and the feeling in her body so intense from the release of these tears that it made her body collapse with relief.

-- Would you like to stop for tonight? Father Ignacio asked her.

-- Father, maybe we can talk again some day, Makaila offered.

Just then Father Ignacio seemed to be staring out into nothing. It seemed that he didn't hear what Makaila just asked. Makaila watched Father Ignacio as he was thinking about something. His eyes shifted from one side to the other and his head tilted down a bit every time he saw something in his mind's eye. Father Ignacio closed his eyes slowly. Makaila could see his chest rise with the heavy sigh Father Ignacio made. Makaila got worried. Her eyes quickly dried as her heartbeat slowly began to speed up.

-- Father? Father Ignacio?, Makaila said trying to get his attention.

-- The room at the top of the stairs.... tell me about the room at the top of the stairs, Father Ignacio asked Makaila with a determined look on his face.

Makaila was dumbfounded. She was scared and at the same time amazed. She herself had forgotten about the room at the top of the stairs that was always closed. A shiver went up her spine at the flood of memories that came about that room; and about Father Ignacio's vision. Makaila hated that room. Every time she passed the locked door, Makaila felt the utmost terror.

Several times Bonnie insisted they sneak into the room when no one was around. In the room, Bonnie dragged Makaila into a closet to listen through a vent to the sounds that came up from the basement. And as much as Makaila tried, she couldn't remember if she heard anything, but a part of her memory seems to have heard horrid screams come up from the basement... through the vent... in the closet.... into the room that they were forbidden to enter.

-- Did Maggie have to go to the Brown's house as much as you did?

-- No, I was the one who went the most. Sometimes Maggie and I would both go, but that wasn't always the case. For some reason, I had to be the one to go over there by myself. And it killed me every time Maggie went there by herself, Makaila responded.

Father Ignacio just shook his head in dismay as Makaila recounted that first time Maggie had to go there by herself.

~ ~ ~

Makaila had contracted Scarlet Fever and was very sick. Makaila's mother was crying outside her door and she overheard her mom tell her father that she was afraid that Makaila was going to die. Makaila felt at that time that her mother really did care and it gave Makaila the will to get better. Since Makaila was sick, it kept her from going over to the Brown's. Being sick was worse on Makaila because it meant that Maggie had to go to the Browns' house instead.... and that killed Makaila. She was so terrified that they would do something to Maggie or that Mr. Brown would take her in the middle of the night like he took Bonnie. Maggie was never the same after that.

Because Makaila was sick, plans to go to Florida with the Brown's was put off. It was the following summer where plans were being made again for Makaila to go with them and she was so afraid; afraid because Bonnie threatened her that they were going to drown her in the ocean. Makaila never told anyone.

~ ~ ~

Makaila started crying again horribly. Such a painful cry came from deep with in her. Father Ignacio watched her as she let out all these emotions. Father Ignacio's concern was centered on Makaila... and now on Maggie. He felt the pain in his own heart as he cried for her as well. They sat there, Makaila trying to catch her breath and tears rolling down Father Ignacio's own face. This time, Father Ignacio did not turn or wipe away the tear that rolled down his cheek. This time he wanted Makaila to know how supportive he was to her story and to her past. After a few minutes of blissful silence, Makaila asked Father Ignacio how he knew about the upstairs room. It was then that Father Ignacio told her about the vision he had last night while praying. It had taken Father Ignacio by surprise as well. While Makaila was describing the Brown's house, Father Ignacio was piecing together the "deja vu" feelings he was having.

-- How was Maggie different after that night? Father Ignacio asked.

-- I don't know, but a small part was stolen from her, Makaila answered.

-- Are you feeling guilt about that Makaila? Father Ignacio asked.

-- No, I just feel that I have to save Maggie. I feel that I am supposed to do something to free her. I feel like I have to get Maggie from behind a locked door and I can't reach her, Makaila replied.

-- When did you two have to stop going over to the Browns' house? Father Ignacio asked.

-- When we were ten or eleven, Makaila answered.

-- How did that happen? Father Ignacio inquired.

-- I don't recall ever having to spend the night there ever again, Makaila said with an absolute smile on her face. "And I didn't have to go to Florida with them either," she continued.

Even though going to the Browns' house stopped, things in their household were changing drastically. Their mother Lalee was drinking more and became a full-blown alcoholic within a year. The scoldings, the drunken rages and yelling were beginning to become a nightly routine. Maggie always seemed to be the scape goat and not that Makaila was saved from any punishments or spankings, but Maggie seemed to get it for no apparent reason.

But the twins continued in their little lives thinking that things were normal and the same time questioning if their home life was a reality. Birthday celebrations had stopped and holiday occasions seemed like they just went through the motions. And even though they were not allowed to go over to the Browns' house, Bonnie and Mrs. Brown would show up at the strangest times in their lives out of nowhere. They were still, somehow, some way involved in their lives and it wasn't until now that Makaila figured that out.

-- How is Maggie doing these days? Father Ignacio asked Makaila.

-- You will be able to ask her yourself Father, she is coming for a visit in a couple of weeks and I am so excited, Makaila said.

-- Do you think she will be able to talk to me about this, like you can? Father Ignacio asked.

-- I have a feeling that Maggie knows more than I do, Father, Makaila answered.

-- Well then, I look forward in meeting the other person who shares your survival, Father Ignacio asked.

Makaila smiled, and with that they both held hands and prayed.

Chapter Eight

Meeting Maggie

Makaila left that evening at around 10:00. Father Ignacio was even more concerned for what was to follow. The evil, the darkness, the fear and the puzzles without pieces that surrounded Makaila's past was now Father Ignacio's present; and the future for them both. He knew there was also another person involved and probably more deeply involved than Makaila. He went to his bedroom that night with the constant racing of thoughts and visions that he encountered that evening. His thoughts were inconclusive as to what the actual manuscript to this mystery was. He knew that Makaila played a huge role and that Maggie an even larger one.

Later that evening, Father Ignacio felt exhausted from the discussion and he felt too overwhelmed to even pray his usual way. He asked God to forgive him for his faults and for things he had failed to do. He prayed for peace, strength, wisdom and knowledge; and protection. He prayed for Makaila and for Maggie both. He prayed for their safety and for God's blessings upon the two. But most importantly he prayed for God's light to be shed upon this road. A road full of fear, a road full of tears, a road full of lies, deceit, control and evil. Father Ignacio just knew in his heart and soul that the spirit of darkness was involved and Father Ignacio's soul had been at guard since this whole thing commenced. He felt strangely empowered, strangely convinced that his help was greatly needed here. He knew that the outcome would rely on his involvement, but what sort of involvement would be needed he was still not convinced about. He no longer felt like he or Makaila had a choice in this matter. He felt destined. He felt that it was certainly out of his control. This was above that. God had driven this course into their live's paths. God's work was being done here and no one could stop God's hand from flourishing.

Father Ignacio rose to his feet from the kneeler in his room. He sat in the wooden chair in front of his desk. The lit candles flame flickered against the wall. He cupped his chin with his hand as his arm and elbow rested on his lap. He brought both of his hands up as they came together in prayer as his fingers rubbed against his forehead and down the bridge of his nose and onto his lips. He closed his eyes in fatique. He needed sleep tonight. He rose from his seat and walked over to his nightstand. He peered out the window onto the garden that was bright with the light of the full moon in the sky. He looked up into the sky as a cloud passed ever so slowly in front of the moon's brilliance. Suddenly a pain struck his heart. A pain so deep, so real and full of no mistake, Father Ignacio was touched again. Touched by the hand of God himself. He felt his mind free up, his soul escape his body. He felt the most supreme love ever. He felt a light envelope him. The fragrance of sweet aroma entered his nostrils as he breathed in a heavy sigh. Father Ignacio smiled, his eyes widened with wonderment at the sight before him. Hills, paths, trees and clouds of gold filled his eyes. His mouth opened in bewilderment and his soul smiled. He quickly removed his white pastoral collar. His breath was hard to catch. He unloosened his shirt collar as his fingers pulled on the fabric around his neck. Sweat glistened on his forehead. He felt the pain in his chest and yet he was not uncomfortable with the feeling. His eyes widened in awe at the sight before him. The huge light quickly dilated his eyes. He reached up as to touch something before him. The smile that left his face was of the most beautiful smile ever. His knees and legs weakened. Sweat was now pouring down the sides of his face. Father Ignacio's eyes rolled back into his head as his body slumped over onto his bed.

Sister Angelica was in her room when Father Ignacio retired to his. Sister felt a little concerned about Father Ignacio tonight. She saw the deep pain he was carrying earlier and Sister Angelica was uneasy about that. She was sitting on her bed, brushing her hair when she heard the not-so-occasional familiar noises in Father Ignacio's bedroom. She slowly stood up from her bed and walked to her door. She slowly turned the knob and her door creaked open. She peeked out down the hall towards Father Ignacio's room. From under his door she saw the glowing light flow out from under it. Sister Angelica crossed herself as she slowly closed the door to her room. She knelt in prayer as her mouth and soft whispers of praises escaped her being. She prayed deeply. She prayed trance-like in her glory to God. She prayed with an almost frightened look on her face. And, she thought to herself, "not again, dear Lord.... not again."

Father Ignacio looked out before him and saw only the whispy clouds of heaven. His body felt light and a disoriented feeling engaged his feelings. He didn't know where he was, where he was going, who he was. The supreme calmness and peace he expereinced engorged his body and mind and the feeling felt great. He felt that all pain and all negative did not exist in this plane. He looked around as his body took flight. Nothing compared to the feeling he was having. He looked down and saw a tiny room, with a bed, a desk and nightstand. He looked closely as confusion entered his thoughts. He glided closer to the vision before him. He saw a man, laying half on the bed and half on the floor. Now more delirious, more confused he descended closer to the sight below him. He felt the pain in his chest again as he he tried to recognize the man on the bed. He felt light-headed and faint. He descended quickly. It was then that he recognized the man below. His eyes widened, his mind cramped with fear as he saw himself as the man before him. His chest hurt even more as his vision was getting darker. He descended faster and faster as his life flashed before him in frames. The light surrounding the tiny room was brighter than before and within a whisk, he no longer hovered above the vision below. He was part of the vision and darkness filled the room.

It was 5:30 in the morning when Sister Angelica rose off her knees. She rubbed her hands together as she massaged them. She looked out her window. The sun had not yet risen and the quiteness of the early morning hour echoed through-out. She got up from her bed and walked to her door. She walked out to the hall and down to Father Ignacio's room. She stood outside his door for a moment, she crossed herself and gently knocked. There was no answer. She slowly turned the knob to his room and she peered in. Father Ignacio was laying half on his bed and his legs touched the floor. She grabbed his legs and lifted them up to the bed. She pulled the blanket that lay across the back of his chair and draped it on him. She looked down on him with somber eyes and she half smiled. His hair was soaking wet and his face was flushed. She brushed his brow with her hand and whispered, "sleep Father, sleep now." She made the sign of the cross on his forehead with her fingers and walked out of his room.

Father Ignacio slept until two o'clock that afternoon. He woke up in his bed and noticied that he had his clothes on from the day before. He felt drained and incoherent for a moment until he realized that he must have fallen asleep during his prayers last night. He walked into his bathroom. He stood in front of the sink as he filled his cupped hands with water and splashed the coolness onto his face. He lifted up and saw his reflection in the mirror as water dripped from his face. He took a second glance and noticied his hair. He stood there dumbfounded. His hair was a little more grayer than usual. He questioned it for a moment as he stared at it almost swearing that it wasn't like that the day before. He walked out into his room and into his closet to retrieve fresh clothes to wear. He peered into the mirror that hung on the inside door of his closet. He turned around and walked over to his nightstand. He picked up a book from the carpeted floor that must have fallen off his nightstand. It was the same book that he had found laying on the floor by his bookshelf a few weeks ago when he knelt in prayer. He looked at the book ever so meticulously, turning from front cover to back cover and feeling the embroidered raised design on the faded leather covering. The pages were inlaid with gold edging as he fingered through the pages. It was his book. A book containing his seminary certificates, awards, degrees and his ordination diploma with the official papal seal. It also contained every degree of ministry he had ever accomplished. From altar boy, to usher, to a Eucharist Minister, Lector, Catechist and Deacon. The second half of the book contained the Latin Mass, special prayers, rites and blessings. A feeling of pride swelled up within him as he thumbed through the pages. Towards the end of the book, he noticed that a few pages had been ripped out or had fallen out. A sinking feeling came over him. He looked on the floor where the book had been and also towards the bookshelf to see if pages had accidentally fallen out. He was sick to his stomach to think that he may have lost some pages to this special book. He also felt shame for not placing this book in a more safe place. It was a passport to his priesthood and not a book for just a bookshelf or coffee table. He found nothing. He held the book tightly to his chest. He walked back into his closet. He knelt down and pulled out a safe lockbox from behind in the corner of his closet. He fumbled for his keys in his pockets and opened up the safe. He smiled as pictures of his family loaded the area within the safe. He noticed his high school diploma and college certificates as well. He gently placed the book in the safe and closed the lid. He locked it and slid it back behind his clothes in the corner. He questioned where those missing pages would be and Father Ignacio was hard on himself as to his carelessness. He asked for forgiveness as he grabbed his fresh clothes and walked to his bathroom and closed the door.

Father Ignacio did not hear from Makaila for a week. He continuely replayed the memories Makaila recounted to him almost every waking minute. He worried about her. And he worried about Maggie. Father Ignacio knew that Maggie knew much more than Makaila could remember; and he didn't know if that was a good thing or not. Father Ignacio felt compelled to speak with Maggie and that confused him and that intrigued him at the same time. He felt the pain that Makaila was experiencing and yet he was determined to ease that hurt for her, for them both, Maggie and her. He was growing more concerned that Makaila had not contacted him in a few days.

Father Ignacio walked into the rectory one morning after morning Mass. He called for Sister Angelica. The offices were quiet and soft praise and worship music played in the background. Sister Angelica did not respond. Father Ignacio walked back towards the living quarters of the rectory and again called for Sister Angelica. No answer came. Father Ignacio wondered were she may have gone. He walked past the kitchen, past the living room and down to his bedroom. When he came approaching Sister Angelica's room, he heard her talking on the phone. Father Ignacio was going to walk past her door when he heard her say the name of Monsignor Kealy. Father Ignacio stopped and though he knew that he should not listen in, he did. Sister Angelica continued to stay on the telephone.

-- Yes, Monsignor Kealy, she said. "It happened again last week. It lasted longer this time...... Be assured that I will Monsignor...... No, he is at morning Mass....... I shall contact you again....... God bless you, Monsignor."

Father Ignacio leaned up against the wall when he heard her hang up the telephone. He quickly went back down the hall and made his way to the kitchen making certain that his steps could not be heard. Father Ignacio grew suspicious. Sister Angelica didn't know Monsignor Kealy and he was certain that's what he heard her say. What was she speaking about? What happened last week that lasted longer than usual? And what was she assuring Monsignor Kealy about? His head began to spin. Something is not right here, he thought. Maybe Monsignor Kealy called and I wasn't here. No, that can't be. Sister Angelica has a private line, he further thought. Why is he worried about it? Sister Angelica might just tell him about the conversation she just had with Monsignor Kealy. Father Ignacio stood in the kitchen and yelled for Sister Angelica as he had just come in.

-- Sister, are you here? Father Ignacio asked.

A few seconds passed. Sister Angelica was walking down the hall in a semi-hurried pace.

-- I'm here, Sister Angelica retorted.

-- I called out a couple of times for you, Father Ignacio said curious to her next response.

-- Oh, I am sorry Father. I was looking for some of my notes from last week's Legion of Mary meeting. Must have not heard you.

She quickly turned away from Father Ignacio and faced the kitchen stove.

-- Want something to eat? Sister Angelica asked.

-- No, no thank you Sister, Father Ignacio replied.

-- Very well then. I'm gonna walk over to the church a little early this morning. Looks like a beautiful day outside for a little stroll, she continued without pausing.

"I will see you later then," Father Ignacio said as Sister Angelica walked past him to the back door. Father Ignacio felt an awful feeling of betrayal, he felt numb. He questioned, he wondered and unfamiliar suspicions ran through his mind. He felt a touch of anger scrape the edges of his emotions and he didn't like it; but mostly, he didn't like the feeling he had about Sister Angelica lying to him.

Most of the day and the next Father Ignacio felt disturbed, but tried hard not make it noticeable to Sister Angelica. Makaila did call a couple days later and this made Father Ignacio lose sight of what transpired with Sister Angelica. Father Ignacio was going to meet Maggie next week. Makaila called to invite Father Ignacio for dinner. Makaila was doing fairly well considering the moments that they spent together that night last week. A lot of hard work and troubled fears, anger, confusion and questioning along with saddened tears accompanied that night and Makaila was as strong as ever. Father Ignacio admired her resilience and prayed that she would continue on this path in that same strength.

~ ~ ~

The rest of the week went by quickly for Father Ignacio but for Makaila it went by extremly slow. She could not wait for Maggie to arrive. It had been a few months since they had seen each other and usually they do not go this long. Makaila woke up the morning of Maggie's arrival feeling excited and happy.

Makaila arrived at the airport a half hour early and grabbed a cup of fancy coffee for both her and Maggie and she waited patiently at the gate. Finally, Maggie's flight was announced and Makaila stood up to greet her other half. Memories of them both as little girls ran through Makaila's mind and an incredible feeling of completeness overwhelmed her.

Out in the distance of the jetway Makaila saw Maggie. Makaila smiled and her eyes jumped for joy. Maggie saw Makaila at the same time and she put a faster step to her walking towards Makaila. Regardless of who and how many people were around, Maggie threw her bag down and they embraced. Their smiles lit up the terminal gate as tears of joy filled their eyes. People slowed down and stared and smiled as they saw the true commitment these two people had with each other and being that they were identical twins, made them even more appreciate the sight before them. Maggie looked at Makaila and Makaila looked at Maggie as if they were separated at birth and not had seen each other in many years. Their special bond and love was obvious. They both had looks on their faces that said 'as long as we had each other, nothing else mattered.' They walked away from the crowd that was emerging from the plane and grabbed a seat at a nearby terminal restaurant.

-- I need a cigarette, Maggie said with a desperate voice. "It was a long flight."

They sat as Maggie opened up the lid to her styrofoam cup of coffee that

Makaila had bought earlier. She reached for some artificial sugar, tore open the package and poured the contents into her coffee. Makaila watched Maggie as she did this and Makaila was joyful at having Maggie at her side. Even though they shared the same face, Makaila had love for her, felt the joy in her heart, sensed the smiles lift her eyes and experienced the incredible surge of true ties and bonds; and Maggie felt the same way.

-- Was it a good flight? Makaila asked Maggie.

-- It was okay, they had a movie, but didn't really watch it. I met this one person I sat next to and we talked almost the whole way over, Maggie said.

-- You know we both get teased about that don't you, Makaila said.

-- About what? Maggie questioned.

-- That we do the opposite of not speaking with strangers, Makaila said smiling.

-- Oh, they can kiss my butt! Maggie jokingly said.

-- Maggie! Makaila said in surprise, even though Maggie had always said off the wall things.

-- What?, Maggie said mischeviously.

Maggie puffed on her cigarette and took a drink from her coffee. Makaila just laughed silently at Maggie's last statement.

-- So did you take the day off today? Maggie asked of Makaila.

-- Yes, actually the whole week, Makaila answered her.

-- You know what? Maggie said as she extinguished her cigarette.

-- What? Makaila answered.

-- I'm gonna pee in my pants if i don't find a restroom soon, Maggie continued.

Makaila just smiled and nodded her head. They rose from the table and headed for the ladie's room where they talked about old boyfreinds, their lives, their jobs, their friends just like they were continuing a discussion from that morning. They didn't skip a beat while enlightening each other with what was going on in their lives. They walked out of the restroom and headed for baggage claim to retrieve Maggie's suitcases. Once there, Maggie introduced Makaila to the lady she sat next to on the flight and it wasn't long before all three were laughing at something that was said. People around them stared at both Maggie and Makaila and even though they have been stared at several times before in their lives, they felt proud and portrayed to the whole world that they liked being twins. Maggie's suitcases were loaded onto a cart as they headed out of the terminal to the parking garage.

-- It's hotter than hell here! Maggie stammered.

-- You'll get used to it, Makaila said as they walked on the asphalt parking garage to her car.

-- When? Maggie asked.

-- When what? Makaila questioned.

-- When will I get used to it! Maggie said as she fanned herself with a magazine she was carrying in her bag.

-- It's not that bad, Makaila said smiling.

-- Like hell it isn't, no pun intended, Maggie said as they both started laughing.

They reached Makaila's car and loaded the suitcases in the trunk and backseat. They crouched into the car as they slapped on their seatbelts.

-- This car better have air conditioning! Maggie said.

-- Stop already, Makaila said laughing. Wanna go for lunch? Makaila continued.

-- You know it, sister of mine, Maggie answered.

They drove out of the parking garage and onto a main highway as they again started talking, continuing where they left off. They were amazing. They knew about each other's lives as much as they were not in them on a daily basis. There was a break in silence before they reached the Mexican restaurant Makaila was taking Maggie to.

-- What will we be doing tomorrow? Maggie asked.

-- Well, Maggie, I've invited Father Ignacio to join us for dinner tomorrow night, Makaila answered.

Maggie grew a bit silent as she stared out the window. Makaila grabbed Maggie's hand.

-- It'll be alright. You will love him. He's a great man, Makiala said trying to comfort Maggie.

-- I know, Maggie replied.

Makaila did not expect the response that Maggie just gave. Her immediate silence had Makaila wondering if she had done the right thing. They reached the restaurant, were escorted to a table, ate their lunch, drank their drink and Father Ignacio was not brought up once.

Later that evening, after Makaila gave the grand tour of her apartment, they sat on the couch, popped in a movie while the smell of popcorn filled the room. Maggie fell asleep almost immediately and Makaila shortly thereafter and the feeling they both felt was of them holding on to each other's nightgowns like many years ago.

~ ~ ~

Father Ignacio was getting ready for his dinner with Makaila and Maggie. He seemed almost anxious to meet Maggie, but certainly felt he needed to go. He wondered if Makaila had shared with Maggie the talks they had so far. He worried about what Maggie would think of him. Would she think that Makaila said too much or what ulterior motives may he have in helping them? He had almost forgotten the incident with Sister Angelica and this dinner invitation came at an appropriate time. Ever since he overheard Sister Angelica on the telephone, she had been extra nurturing to him, extra helpful, more concerned and if Father Ignacio didn't know any better, a little more protective. Father Ignacio decided to put that incident in the back of his mind to deal with later; if he felt he needed to. Even though Father Ignacio was anxious to meet Makaila and Maggie, he also felt curious. Makaila had spoken so much of Maggie that he felt he knew her and Father Ignacio didn't know if that would make Maggie uncomfortable. As he drove in his car he prayed for God's guidance and wanted to make certain that he make a good first impression.

~ ~ ~

At the table, Makaila and Maggie sat. Makaila seemed excited that Maggie was finally going to meet Father Ignacio and Maggie felt as though she was going to meet the Pope. Maggie seemed a little on edge as she nervously drank her iced tea with Makaila who was making small talk and Maggie replying with one-word responses. Maggie lit up a cigarette. She took in a deep puff as she exhaled the smoke.

-- Maybe we should have sat in the non-smoking section? Maggie asked Makaila.

-- No, it's quite alright. Father Ignacio smokes, Makaila responded.

-- Are you sure it's okay? Maggie continued.

-- Yes, It's fine. He would probably love it. You already have something in common, Makaila smiled as she said this.

-- Is this seat taken?

Makaila recognized Father Ignacio's voice as he snuck up from behind them. Maggie quickly put out her cigarette as Makaila was standing up to greet her friend. She gave Father Ignacio a hug. Maggie stood up to meet the person Makaila thought so highly of.

-- How are you Makaila? Father Ignacio asked her.

-- I am fine Father, Makaila said smiling. This..... this is my twin sister Maggie, she continued with the biggest smile ever.

Father Ignacio held out his hand to Maggie. Maggie smiled and took his hand in hers and smiled.

-- How are you Father? Nice to finally meet you, Maggie said.

-- I am fine... Makaila has told me so much about you. I feel like I know you and by the looks of things I knew what you would look like, Father Ignacio said as he smiled.

-- Quite clever Father, Maggie replied as they laughed a light-hearted laugh together.

-- Do you think we look alike, Father? Makaila asked.

-- Quite uncanny. Very special indeed, Father Ignacio continued. Please sit, he continued.

Maggie, Makaila and Father Ignacio sat at the table. Father Ignacio couldn't resist staring at the similar faces that smiled in unison. Even though he knew which one was Makaila, he felt that he couldn't tell them apart. Makaila just smiled and stood with pride that Father Ignacio liked Maggie so far. Maggie looked at Makaila and at Father Ignacio. Immediately Maggie felt what Makaila felt when she first met him. Her defenses went down a few notches and her body relaxed in comfort. Maggie glanced at Makaila and smiled a smile that said, "I see what you are talking about." They both smiled at each other with their eyes in only a way that twins would only know how. Father Ignacio and Makaila themselves also communicated non-verbally to each other that seemed to have said, "everything will be fine.... we can go on from here and conquer whatever needs conquering." They had a pleasant evening and Father Ignacio finally met the other survivor; and together their spirits danced a dance of joy; and Father Ignacio saw that vision clearly.

Chapter Nine

Maggie

Father Ignacio went home that evening with such a happy heart. Seeing Makaila and Maggie together was a welcoming sight and Father Ignacio knew that their bond was strong and unbreakable. He also felt anger again as he recounted the many stories Makaila discussed with him on how people try to separate them. Looking back at it, Father Ignacio felt that people were threatened by their special bond, their naiveness, their innocence, their spirits; but those people who really wanted to separate them like the Browns had other plans for them. Plans that Father Ignacio wasn't quite sure about yet, but with Maggie's help, he felt positive that a little more light was to be shed on the subject. At dinner that night he felt amazed at the similarities and yet the differences between Makaila and Maggie. It was amazing how they smiled alike, how they held their silverware the same and how they fashioned their eyes when they talked. It was like looking into a mirror and seeing them both interact with each other was a treat. They have been blessed and Father Ignacio was certain that they were especially created. It made Father Ignacio even sadder that they have a story to tell. He felt it in his heart. He felt it in his soul; and he was ready. He was ready for Maggie to fill in the blanks and finish off the story yet untold and yet unspoken.

Makaila called Father Ignacio a couple of days later.

-- Father Ignacio, I have spoken with Maggie and she wants to say hello, Makaila said.

-- Father? Maggie inquired.

-- Yes, Maggie how are you? Father Ignacio asked.

-- I'm fine Father, I am ready to meet with you though, Maggie said almost tearfully.

Father Ignacio was taken back a little at Maggie's forwardness. Even though he welcomed the opportunity to hear her story and decipher the events that transpired at their young age, he also felt anxiety enter his body.

-- Father? Are you there? Maggie asked.

-- Yes, Maggie, I'm here, Father Ignacio responded. When would you like to get together? He asked.

-- I'm gonna leave that up to Makaila. Would you mind making the plans with her? Maggie asked.

-- No, not at all, Father Ignacio answered.

-- Well, here's my sister, Father, thank you, Maggie said.

-- Maggie, not to worry... things will be more than fine, Father Ignacio calmly said.

-- I know Father, I trust that it will, Maggie said. Here is my sister, good night Father, she continued.

-- Good night Maggie, Father Ignacio said.

-- Father, Hi, this is Makaila.

-- Makaila, hello... so, when would you like to get together? Father Ignacio asked.

After making definite plans to meet in a couple of days, Father Ignacio felt a shudder on his spine. He immediately knew that the forces of evil did not like what was going to happen or transpire. Father Ignacio felt his soul jump within him as a testimony that all would be well. God's blessings will be on them all.

-- God is with us right, Father? Makaila asked.

-- More than you know Makaila, more than you know, Father Ignacio stressed in confidence.

~ ~ ~

Father Ignacio decided to meet them at Makaila's apartment when they made plans to get together; and those couple of days went by quickly. The incident with Sister Angelica seemed unimportant now. Father Ignacio's feelings seemed to have dissipated and he questioned that. Father Ignacio figured that maybe he didn't hear what he heard; either that or he was in complete denial. Nevertheless, God had wiped it out of his conscience and Father Ignacio felt that more important matters were at hand.

Father Ignacio arrived at Makaila's apartment at around 6:00 in the evening.

He stood outside her door when he muttered a Latin prayer under his breath. He prayed it for himself and prayed it for both Maggie and Makaila. The doorbell rang and Maggie answered.

-- Father, so glad you are here, Maggie said with a half-smile.

-- How are you Maggie? Father Ignacio asked her.

-- I am fine. Please come in. Makaila will be right out, Maggie answered.

-- Makaila has a nice place here, Father said as he admired Makaila's decor and furniture.

-- Please Father, have a seat. Can I get you anything to drink? Maggie asked.

-- Maybe a glass of water if that's not too much trouble, Father Ignacio requested.

-- No trouble at all. I should be getting you a five gallon container of water with all the help you have given Makaila, Maggie said.

-- It is my pleasure Maggie, Makaila is a special creature as I am sure you are, Father Ignacio replied.

Maggie walked into the small kitchen that separated the dining area and the living room. She reached up and pulled down a glass from inside a cabinet.

-- So Makaila has told you of our times together? Father Ignacio asked Maggie.

-- Yes she has, Maggie responded with her back to Father Ignacio as she poured ice-cubes into his glass of water.

-- And what do you think? Father Ignacio continued to ask.

-- I am not as strong as Makaila Father. I hope I can speak to you as Makaila speaks with you, Maggie sheepishly answered.

-- You will be amazed how much strength God gives us when we desperately need it, Father Ignacio said.

Maggie turned around and just smiled at Father Ignacio when Makaila stepped out of her bedroom.

-- Father, so good to see you again, Makaila said as she reached over to hug him.

-- Hello Makaila, lovely place you have here, Father Ignacio complemented.

-- Thank you Father, please sit down, Makaila insisted.

-- Thanks Makaila, Father Ignacio replied.

Father Ignacio sat on the couch that faced the kitchen. Maggie walked towards him with the glass of water in hand.

-- Here you go Father, Maggie said handing him the glass.

-- Thank you, Father Ignacio said.

-- I bought some dessert earlier today and I thought I would make a pot of coffee for later, Makaila said.

-- Actually I made the dessert. I just boxed it in grocery store packaging to make it look good, Maggie jokingly said.

-- She did not. Don't listen to her Father, Makaila shouted.

-- On the contrary, I do want to listen to Maggie today, Father Ignacio said smiling.

Maggie stopped smiling and felt that she had found her match and someone who was as brazen as her. Maggie was speechless and did not know what to say when Makaila spoke up.

-- Well, since it is a beautiful evening, we have set up a nice table out in the patio and both you and Maggie can smoke up a storm, Makaila mentioned.

-- That's sounds like a great idea. Join me for a cigarette Maggie? Father Ignacio asked her.

-- Um, yes, certainly, Father, Maggie answered.

-- You guys go on out and I'll get dessert ready, Makaila said.

-- Shall we Maggie? Father Ignacio asked her.

Maggie smiled and walked out showing Father Ignacio the way. Makaila was busily getting dishes from the cabinets. When Father Ignacio walked past her, she gave him a smile and a nod. Father Ignacio touched her shoulder and continued out to the patio. Makaila was right. The evening was a perfect temperature. Smells of flowers and candles were evident on the patio. The sun was just about setting as both Maggie and Father Ignacio stared out into it. Father Ignacio reached into his coat pocket and took out the pack of cigarettes. He shook it in a fashion that made one of the cigarettes slide up. He offered it to Maggie.

-- Thank you Father, Maggie responded.

-- My pleasure, Father Ignacio answered through closed lips as a cigarette dangled from his mouth.

He reached into his pocket again and retrieved his lighter. He flicked it and the yellow-bluish flame lightened the now darkening patio. He offered it to Maggie who leaned in while he lit her cigarette. Father Ignacio pulled back when smoke from Maggie's cigarette was visible. He brought the flame to his own face as he cocked his head to one side to light his cigarette. He puffed in heavily and exhaled the smoke out into the air. He slipped his lighter into his pants pocket as they both stared at the sunset. Smoke lingered in the air above them as a sort of camaraderie was certain between them as smokers.

Father, you know I am really nervous, don't you? Maggie finally spoke up.

-- Are you nervous about me? Father Ignacio asked apologetically.

-- Well, no, and yes, Maggie said.

-- And why is that? Father Ignacio asked.

-- I don't know.... maybe because I know what's going to happen, Maggie continued.

-- What do you think will happen? Father Ignacio inquired.

-- I am afraid to say things that I have suppressed many years ago, Maggie said.

-- Do you know why you would want to keep them suppressed? Father Ignacio asked.

-- Because it is so hard. The horror that fills my body when I recount what I remember is almost too much to bear, Maggie said with choked words.

-- You know, someone once told me that trauma victims should recount their stories as much as they can to as many people as they can, Father Ignacio lectured. Do you know why that is? he continued.

--No, Father, why is that, Maggie said with a little more comfort to her body.

-- The more you recount, the less it is suppressed and the less traumatic it becomes. Human beings should not carry in their subconscious things that are not of God. It clouds our every move, our every direction in life, our focus for living. The less things suppressed, the lighter our world becomes, Father Ignacio said without a pause and with a purpose.

Maggie smiled. Her defenses shattered. Her fears lifted away. Maggie felt what Makaila was talking about. She saw what Makaila described. She was touched by Father Ignacio and not because he was a priest but much more than that. She felt close to a person for the first time in a different way than most people feel. Maggie felt lighter. Her thoughts became unclouded and worries of feeling traumatized were wiped away. "What is it about this man that makes you melt in peace?" she thought. "What is it that you felt compelled to say it all, with no remorse of embarrassment or judgement?" she continued to wonder. Maggie looked into his eyes and saw what Makaila saw, his eyes were full of heaven; nothing else that she has ever experienced came close to her feeling at this moment; and Maggie liked it; and Maggie couldn't wait to tell Makaila that she was right. Father Ignacio smiled back at Maggie and was pleased that God had blessed him with a good first impression. He felt Maggie's soul ease off a little from being on guard and he was amazed that the spirit that held Makaila so strong was identical to Maggie's. It was at this time that Father Ignacio understood now the differences and the similarities between the two. He reminded himself of the conversations he had with Makaila about Maggie. He remembered that Makaila said that Maggie was a little more brazen then she was; but what hit Father Ignacio like a ton of bricks was that Makaila was bold too. In this very short time of meeting Maggie he knew that they were indeed very special. Maggie was certainly brazen and Makaila..... well, it was Makaila's soul that is brazen. Father Ignacio was choked up with this thought that he felt a lump in his throat when he further put it together. These two women, these two creatures of God were unique in their being. Unique in their survival, unique spirits blessed by the very hand of God. One....Maggie, protected their outside world by being brazen, while the other one, Makaila, protected their spirits by her brazen soul. What a most beautiful kinship, what a beautiful relationship, what a beautiful testimony of God's remarkable work.

-- I don't know where to begin, Maggie spoke breaking the tiny space of silence.

-- Well, I think we start with a cup of coffee, Father Ignacio said smiling as Makaila walked out with a tray of cups, saucers and spoons.

-- You're my kinda guy Father, Maggie retorted.

-- Ready for coffee I see, Makaila said as she placed the tray on the table.

-- Smells great, Makaila, Father Ignacio replied.

-- Good, I have a lot more in the kitchen, Makaila said as she pulled out a chair for Father Ignacio and Maggie.

-- Your gonna have coffee with us right Makaila? Maggie asked.

-- Well, yes, I can't have you have all the fun, Makaila responded smiling a smile at Maggie that seemed to say. "I told you..."

-- You forgot the dessert, Maggie teasingly said.

-- I figured you can get it, Makaila teased back.

-- Well fine then, Maggie said as she stood up and walked into the kitchen. Makaila just smiled at Father Ignacio and at Maggie.

Maggie walked out and Makaila leaned in closer to Father Ignacio and she whispered, "isn't she great!" Father Ignacio smiled and said "yes indeed. What a special bond you two have." He thought of telling Makaila what he just thought about. His analogy of their strength and their protection for each other. He further thought that it should be left for another time. He looked at Makaila who was dancing inside and looked as giddy as young girl. Father Ignacio knew that Makaila was pleased that Maggie was so comfortable with him. And Makaila couldn't figure out why Maggie wouldn't be.

-- Dessert coming right up, Maggie said in a raised voice with the tray of cheesecake over her head.

-- Ah, is this the dessert you slaved all day to make? Father Ignacio teasingly asked Maggie.

-- Yup, I even slid in the little waxed papers in between each slice myself, Maggie said as they all laughed together in the silence of the early evening.

~ ~ ~

They had a grand time having their dessert and coffee and watching the rest of the sun set behind the westerly mountains in the horizon. Maggie was more comfortable with every passing moment and Makaila flourished at Maggie's and Father Ignacio's connection. Makaila looked at her watch. Forty-five minutes had passed. She got up and fetched another pot of coffee from inside the kitchen while she picked up the dishes and forks from their desserts. She looked at Maggie who was sitting directly in front of Father Ignacio. Makaila gave her look that had said, "I'm gonna leave you alone with Father Ignacio and Maggie looked back as if she said, "that would be fine."

-- Well, Makaila said drawing in a heavy sigh, "I have some work to do for my class next week." So I'll leave you two alone to chitchat, she continued.

-- Thank you for the coffee Makaila, Father Ignacio said.

-- My pleasure Father, Makaila said with a smile.

-- And don't fall asleep in there, Maggie teased Makaila.

Makaila left the outside patio. Clinking dishes were heard from inside as she rinsed them. Father Ignacio reached for a cigarette. Maggie spoke.

-- I don't know what I would do without Makaila. She is my biggest supporter, Maggie said breaking the silence.

--She says the same about you, Father Ignacio replied.

-- We have been lost many times in our lives and if it wasn't for each of us, I don't know where we would be now, Maggie said.

-- That's very obvious, but you would never be too lost, Father Ignacio replied.

-- What makes you so certain? Maggie questioned him.

-- Just a feeling. A kind of "knowing." You two were born with a special destiny, Father Ignacio recited.

-- Growing up, we never thought so. We were faced with two realities.

132

-- And those realities would be? Father Ignacio pressed her.

-- One reality.... that everything was fine, Maggie said.

-- And the other? Father Ignacio inquired.

-- that everything was not..... Maggie said almost sinking into her chair.

-- There is another reality, Father Ignacio sternly said.

-- Another reality? Maggie questioned as her eyebrows raised.

-- God's reality, Father Ignacio said. "A reality that we do not know of, or know the outcome of. It's the reality that God sees and only Him. You see, it's our conscience state that sees and deals with the reality in front of us and it's our soul and spirit that guides God's reality for us", he continued.

-- I wish I knew that a long time ago, Maggie replied.

-- It's not something that we can control, Father Ignacio insisted.

-- And I'm used to that, Maggie angrily said.

-- Meaning? Father Ignacio questioned.

-- It felt that people controlled us when we were children, Maggie continued.

-- Who? Your parents? The Browns? Father Ignacio said without warning.

Maggie looked surprised even though Makaila told her that she had told him almost everything. She just thought it weird that someone else than Makaila would be talking to her about the people mentioned.

-- So tell me about your parents? Father Ignacio asked.

-- Makaila has told you about our parents hasn't she? Maggie questioned.

-- Yes, but I want to hear about Maggie's parents, Father Ignacio cleverly said.

Maggie reached to the center of the patio table and took hold of her cigarette case. She lit one as she leaned back into her chair. Father Ignacio noticed that she took a more reserved stance when the questioning began. He felt confident that she would open up and begin to tell her story; and he felt ready for it.

-- Well, I never had that trust bond with Mom like Makaila has, Maggie said almost somber like.

-- Did you want that "bond" with your mother? Father Ignacio asked.

-- I did and I didn't. I mean, I always felt angry that I was pawned off on Makaila when mom said that Makaila was my "little mother." Mom was supposed to be my mom, not Makaila, she continued. I always felt like Makaila was mom's favorite.

-- And what did you do then? How did you cope? Father Ignacio asked.

-- I hid in humor. I was always the funny one. No one ever took me seriously, except Makaila, Maggie said.

-- Is that all you did to cope? Father Ignacio asked.

-- That's all I remember I did. What else could I have done? Maggie sternly asked. I do remember that I was a crabby child... an angry child. Everyone kept telling me to control my anger and I was teased and you know what Father, with all the jokes and all the antics, I wasn't laughing, Maggie said with tears in her eyes. "I'm still angry, I'm still sad," Maggie said drying her eyes with the napkin she picked up from the table.

-- That's good Maggie.... we don't want to suppress those feelings, Father Ignacio counseled.

-- I did have one bit of control though, Maggie said.

-- And what was that? Father Ignacio asked.

-- I insisted that I be called Maggie and not Margaret. I almost demanded it. Why do you think that I was so adamant about that Father, Maggie asked.

-- I believe that it was the one thing that belonged to you and only you, and if you had control of it, you felt okay. The other stuff rolled off your back and you could deal with that, Father Ignacio answered.

-- That makes sense, I guess, Maggie replied.

-- What about your father?, Father Ignacio continued. What was he like?

Maggie took in a deep breath. She settled into her chair. Father Ignacio noticed that she took on a more serious face when he asked about her dad.

-- Dad, always seemed to be angry about something. Something always seemed to bother him and it wasn't us. It was something else, Maggie said with pity in her voice.

-- You trusted you father more? Father Ignacio asked.

-- Well, yeah, he was dad; but he wasn't innocent, Maggie said.

Father Ignacio looked puzzled.

-- Whatever mom said, dad believed. She would set us up to get in trouble and she had no empathy that we got in trouble. It didn't bother her one bit. Dad loved mom, there is no doubt about that. I think she set us up to hate dad and dad never questioned it much, Maggie said. I think she set up dad to hate Grandma Bella. I think mom told him stories about grandma that weren't true, Maggie continued.

-- So your dad did the punishing? Father Ignacio asked.

-- More like the bad spankings and sometimes for something we didn't know anything about, Maggie said. " He loved mom and I feel that he was in such conflict about mom's problems," Maggie replied.

-- Problems? What sort of problems? Father Ignacio asked.

-- Mom was an alcoholic and she was addicted to prescription medications. She had serious mental problems that all seemed to have started out of nowhere, Maggie said almost in tears.

At that time Makaila walked back out to what had seemed to be after many hours. Father Ignacio watched Makaila look at Maggie. He was amazed how they said so many words without saying a thing. Maggie motioned Makaila to sit next to her.

-- How are things going? Makaila asked.

-- I was just telling Father Ignacio about mom, about her addictions, Maggie said.

-- Oh, mom was quite ill after a certain point in our lives, Makaila said almost embarrassed.

-- Maggie mentioned mental problems? What was that like? Father questioned the two.

Maggie and Makaila both almost hid their face. Father Ignacio felt that he may have been too strong in asking this question. They both were vulnerable to talk about their mother's mental state.

One thing was clear is that they both agreed that it started very subtly and after the Browns' were no longer in their lives. They both recounted the stories of when Lalee was placed in an institution for a mental breakdown. They conveyed the dysfunction and the delusional episodes that their mother went through. Lalee was placed there three times within their lives. And they both wholeheartedly agreed that their father was completely in denial about his wife's condition; and when he wasn't in denial, he blamed them for not loving their mother enough and that was the reason Lalee was sick. "If only you loved your mom enough, she wouldn't be sick," he would say.

Both Makaila and Maggie always resented it when their father said that to them. They were angry with him and at the same moment, felt pity and sadness that he didn't see beyond his love and denial of Lalee's condition.

Talking about their mothers problems made them feel vulnerable, they felt embarrassed. Father Ignacio felt compassion on the contrary. How these two women turned out to be a special pair; regardless of their past, regardless of their ultimate "safe" persons that said "I tried to get rid of you as kids and it didn't work," to the other saying, "if you loved your mother more, she wouldn't be sick" was a miracle in itself. Again Father Ignacio's heart opened and a fresh wound existed.

Chapter Ten

Maggie's Memories

Maggie, Makaila and Father Ignacio noticed how quickly the evening came and they all shared another cup of coffee. Maggie looked a little drained from the already difficult questions and conversation they had. Makaila squeezed Maggie's hand under the table. Father Ignacio looked up into the darkening sky.

-- It's amazing how the Lord gives us just enough of what we can handle, Father Ignacio finally spoke.

-- That's a good thing, Maggie said.

-- Yes, but sometimes we don't know what we can handle until after we have gotten through it, Father Ignacio replied.

-- I guess you're right about that Father, Makaila finally piped in.

They all smiled at each other as the distant lights of the city were shining bright in the horizon. Inside Makaila's apartment the telephone rang. Makaila excused herself as she made her way around the table and chairs and ran into the house. Maggie and Father Ignacio heard her say her salutation "hello" as she picked up the receiver. Father Ignacio looked at Maggie and offered her a cigarette. Maggie reached over and took one out of his pack. She lit it as Father Ignacio lit his.

-- And how was home life? Father Ignacio asked.

-- Home life? What do you mean? How things were at home? Maggie questioned.

-- Yes, what was it like at home? Father Ignacio replied.

-- At what age Father? Maggie questioned him.

-- All ages. What comes to mind immediately when I ask you this question? Father Ignacio said.

-- Popcorn and Coke, Maggie said out of no where. I can remember that the Friday nights of popcorn and Coke stopped all of a sudden, Maggie said.

-- Is that all that changed? Father Ignacio asked.

Maggie sat there in the midst of all these questions. Her mind wandered back. The age where the popcorn, Coke, birthday parties stopped. Also where her mother's illness, her drinking, the strange people around them, the Browns, Bonnie, her father's anger, her crabbiness, her inner anger, people not taking her serious enough started. Maggie wanted to leave that part of her memory locked away because of the constant confusing messages she received as a child. On one hand they looked like the average middle class Americans and the All- American family. What happened behind closed doors is something that both Maggie and Makaila wanted to leave back there.

Maggie remembered that things started turning for the worse when her braids were cut off and she also had no recollection of when that was. She and Makaila played together. They were each other's safe place to go. They both believed in themselves and in each other and they tried hard to not let anyone separate them. Maggie remembers the torment of when their mother would constantly trim their bangs and she always did that when she had one too many drinks. Maggie would cry herself to sleep wishing and praying that her bangs would grow back by morning. Of course they never did. Maggie felt the pain in her heart, the low self-esteem she felt as a child and the constant labeling that she didn't do something right. Along with the mental anguish she felt, she also felt the physical pain she had gone through. Like Makaila, Maggie had physical health symptoms almost unheard of at such a young age. Makaila had scarlet fever and almost died while Maggie had freak accidents and illnesses. Father Ignacio noticed Maggie's body stiffen up as she explained this. Maggie recalled one day where she had an abscessed tooth and that her mother Lalee told the dentist that she had fallen on a Coke bottle. Maggie often wondered why her mother made that story up and told the dentist that's what happened. "She always lied about things like that. I think she was hiding something." Maggie said.

-- Why do you think she did that, Father Ignacio asked.

Maggie's face became angry. Her voice trembled as she said;

-- She was trying to protect herself from getting caught!

-- Caught from what? Father Ignacio pressed.

Maggie's stature changed. Her body straightened up, her eyes gazed off into the distance as she was trying to remember something. "She tried to kill us, she tried to kill us..." Maggie shouted into the outside air. Father Ignacio jumped back a bit as he didn't expect her outburst. Makaila came running out into the patio. "Maggie! What's wrong? Who's trying to kill us? Makaila looked scared and worried at what Maggie had just said. Father Ignacio quickly looked up at Makaila and put up his hand to stop Makaila. Makaila just looked at Maggie in fright. her eyes swelled up with tears. Maggie continued.

-- *We went shopping one day. Makaila and me. Mom took us. We were so excited. Mom had not taken us shopping in such a long time. We pulled out of the driveway and we thought it strange for a moment that we weren't going in the usual way. But we continued to play and scream and giggle with excitement. We headed down towards the hill when mom pushed on her brakes and said that it looked like rain and she needed to close the upstairs window to our bedroom. Again we thought that was strange since there wasn't a cloud in the sky. Mom walked out and closed the door as she walked to the house. Within moments the car started rolling down the hill. It was a big hill and at the end of it was a busy intersection.*

Makaila screamed under her breath as her hand covered up her screams. Tears were now rolling down her cheek. Maggie turned around and faced Makaila.

-- Do you remember that? Maggie asked her.

-- I do now, Makaila said trying to catch her breath and reaching for a paper napkin.

Makaila walked over to Maggie to hug her. Father Ignacio remembered the words that Makaila said to him a couple of weeks ago. *"I tried to get rid of you kids, but it never worked."* Father Ignacio choked on trying to catch his own breath after he recalled the words that their mother said to them at one point in their lives. Father Ignacio's heart ached at the thought of what they must have felt when she spoke these words to them. Makaila and Maggie were tight in their embrace with each other. Makaila kept whispering in Maggie's ear, "I remember, I remember."

After a brief silence, they both continued how an elderly lady walking along the sidewalk noticed the car rolling down the hill and shouted at them to apply the brakes. They remembered how their mother didn't react as much at the thought that they could have all been killed.

-- What did your father do? Father Ignacio asked them both.

Maggie couldn't remember and Makaila couldn't either, if their father ever knew what had happened.

Both Makaila and Maggie held onto each other and Father Ignacio was touched by their unconditional bond. Without a word being spoken they both supported each other and there was no doubt in their mind that they wouldn't believe one another when one spoke of things that was obviously so painful.

-- Are you both okay? Father Ignacio asked sympathatically.

-- We're okay Father, Makaila answered between sobs.

Maggie held onto Makaila and it was clear to Father Ignacio that Maggie had a lot more to deal with when it came to their story. Makaila loved Maggie and that was all that Maggie ever needed... and so did Makaila.... and they both were confident that they would always get that from each other. Makaila looked at Maggie with the most saddest eyes Father Ignacio had ever seen.

-- Maggie, I never would have remembered that. Have you always remembered that?, Makaila asked.

-- I just remembered it now. It was so clear and so vivid. I had not remembered it before, Maggie answered.

-- It's so clear now. Mom tried to kill us, Makaila said under her breath, but loud enough for Father Ignacio to hear.

Father Ignacio sunk into his chair that seemed to be getting a little uncomfortable now. He, for the life of him, could not believe what he was hearing. A mother, trying to kill her children and he believed them whole-heartedly. Who could do such a thing? What could possess a person, a mother to do away with her own children? Father Ignacio's hairs stood up on his arms... he felt an evil chill through his body. He believed Makaila and Maggie, but still wasn't convinced that their mother wasn't controlled by forces more powerful than her. Father Ignacio rose to his feet and leaned against the railing that separated Makaila's patio from that of the small yard. Father Ignacio placed his hands in his coat pockets and wrapped his coat around him as he crossed his ankles.

-- Father, would you like to go inside? You must be tired sitting in that chair, Makaila asked him.

-- No, this is fine. I just had to stretch for a little bit.

Father Ignacio looked at the patio lamp above and just thought for a minute as he realized how good it felt to stand and let his blood circulate down to his legs and feet. Maggie had kept quiet most of this time and Father Ignacio grew concerned.

-- Maggie are you alright?

Maggie straightened up and looked at Makaila and then at Father Ignacio.

-- I'm fine Father, just embarrassed.

-- Why embarrassed?, he asked her.

-- Well, I usually just don't scream out stuff like that, Maggie answered him.

Makaila placed her hand on Maggie's shoulder. Maggie reached up and placed her hand on Makaila's and smiled.

-- So you never done anything like that before? He asked her.

-- No, not really. I mean, sometimes, I would be doing things at home, and something would pop in my head, like I was trying to remember something... and I tried hard to consciously remember and the more I tried the further it went away.

-- Maybe you shouldn't try to remember, maybe you should just ignore it and see what happens, Father Ignacio offered.

Father Ignacio was feeling drained, but he couldn't leave just yet. He felt that Maggie wanted to say more.

-- Maggie, this may sound a little hard for you to hear and answer, but I would like to know.

-- What's that Father?

Father Ignacio returned to his seat and took a sip of coffee. He looked at Makaila and then at Maggie.

-- Do you remember anyone else trying to hurt you?

Maggie sat there contemplating Father Ignacio's question. Makaila sat next to her and held her hand. Maggie grew silent. Father Ignacio changed the question.

-- Did you play by yourself much? He asked.

-- No, Makaila and I were inseparable. We played together ninety-eight percent of the time, she answered him.

-- What about when Makaila had to go to the Brown's?

Maggie looked off into the distant as to if trying to roll back the pages of time.

-- I have no recollection of where I was, when Makaila left me, Maggie answered almost angry like.

-- When she left you? Father Igancio questioned.

-- Father, I had this overwhelming feeling of abandonment whenever Makaila went over to Bonnie's. I know it's not true, but I felt it. I always questioned why she would leave me. I was lost without her.

Makaila squeezed Maggie's hand tighter as to say, "I would never leave you..." and Maggie reciprocrated.

-- Did you ever have to go to the Brown's house without Makaila?

-- Sometimes..... Maggie said almost zombie-like.... Sometimes...

Father Ignacio looked into the night as if searching for answers. He took up his coffee cup up to his lips and drank the remaining coffee. He knew that Maggie was holding something back. He thought that she was probably trying to protect Makaila from hearing the story. Makaila sensed that Maggie wanted to talk with him alone for a minute. Makaila came out of her daze and asked if anybody wanted more coffee or something else to drink. Father Ignacio asked for a glass of water. He noticied and sensed his dry mouth and lips and a glass of water sounded like a refreshingly good idea.

-- I'll be right back then, Maggie would you like something? Makaila asked.

-- No, I'm fine. Thank you.

Makaila walked into the apartment. When she was out of sight, Maggie leaned in closer to Father Ignacio.

-- Even though Bonnie had a lot more control over Makaila, the most traumatic things happened when Makaila wasn't there, Maggie whispered. They all had it in for Makaila, especially Mr. Brown.

-- What kind of things? What exactly do you mean?

-- Well for instance, they didn't take me to the country as much as they did Makaila. I can also remember when Mr. Brown would come home from work and would walk up to a cabinet. There was a paddle in this cabinet and Mr. Brown always threatened Makaila and never Bonnie when they were getting a little rowdy. We were petrifed of that cabinet and what was in it, Maggie recounted.

-- And you? What traumatic things happened when you were by yourself at the their house? Father Ignacio asked.

Maggie grew silent. She rested back into her chair and lit up a cigarette. This time Maggie offered Father Ignacio one. Father Ignacio took it and lit it. Just then Makaila walked in with a glass and a pitcher of iced water. She placed it on the table and asked if everything was okay. Both Maggie and Father Igancio acknowledged that it was.

-- Well then, I'm going to go inside and finish up on some work, Makaila added.

-- We should be done shortly, Makaila, Father Ignacio commented.

-- It's fine, really.

Makaila walked back into her apartment, this time closing the door to the back patio. Maggie looked out into the distance as if she were watching a movie. She began to pick up where she let off.

-- Father I hated going over there. Bonnie was her meanest to me. She was always nice when Makaila was around, but when we were alone together, she was mean. She just was cruel. Everytime she felt threatened that I was going to tell on something she did, she would crush my fingers when she took hold of my hand. I can remember one time, when she shoved me in a dryer and almost put it on. I was so scared.

-- Did you ever tell? Tell anyone about what Bonnie did to you?

-- Who could I tell? My mother tried to kill us, my dad was in complete denial, Makaila knew, and I certainly didn't feel like I could tell Mr. and Mrs. Brown for fear of what Bonnie would do to me.... or what they would do to me.

Maggie clammed up almost immediately. Her eyes shifted from side to side. She itched in her chair and looked like she had just seen a phantom. Father Ignacio knew that this was the point where Maggie was completely fearful about. But she was ready to talk, she was ready to tell someone what she experienced as a child... and Father Ignacio felt certain that it was something more traumatic than what she had already told.

-- What are you remembering, Maggie?

There was silence.

-- Maggie, what about Mr. & Mrs. Brown? He pressured her into answering.

-- She was always in the kitchen, Mrs. Brown, she was always in the kitchen.

Father Ignacio listen more attentively. This part of Maggie's story has her tied up inside and her retelling this was going to free her a bit, but he felt that it wouldn't free her completely.

-- And you never saw her face. She always had her backed turned to us. I think when I fell off my bike that one day, was the only time I really saw her face.

-- What about Mr. Brown? Father Ignacio said without missing a step.

Maggie grew deathly silent.

-- What about Mr. Brown, Father Ignacio asked again.

-- I hated Mr. Brown, Maggie finally spoke. I hate him, I hate him!! Please no more, please... I hate him!...

Father Ignacio melted into his chair and his heart sank deeper into his chest. He watched Maggie as she transcended into a little girl. He reached out and held her hand. Maggie shook in her chair. Her eyes widened with fear and hatred.

-- Tell me Maggie, tell me about Mr. Brown! Father Ignacio insisted and as much as he hated to bring this about on Maggie he felt it important.

-- I can remember him taking Bonnie in the middle of the night and in the morning Bonnie would be in bed with Mr. Brown, Maggie said stumbling on every word that came from her mouth.

-- Did he ever do anything to you? Father Ignacio continued.

Maggie's face now showed a stream of tears rolling down her cheek. Her body shook with every passing memory that flooded her mind. She held on tightly to Father Ignacio's hand. Maggie recounted the day that Bonnie walked into her father's bedroom and opened up the cedar chest that sat at the foot of his bed and took out a rifle. Maggie cowered as she remembered that she had pointed it at her. Maggie started screaming when her memories recounted the day that Mr. Brown had hit her in the head with a board. She remembered that Mrs. Brown was in the kitchen mixing oils of some sort. Maggie clenched her fists and pounded on the table. Maggie was lost in the Brown's house and she couldn't get out. Father Ignacio remembered that Makaila had told him that she always felt that she needed to get Maggie but couldn't find the door where she was kept. Maggie started screaming for Makaila and her father. Father Ignacio held on to her tighter as she left the patio table back to the Brown's house right before his eyes.

-- No, no, no!!!! Maggie screamed.

-- Where are you Maggie? Father Ignacio said back to her in a raised tone of voice.

151

-- Makaila!!! Makaila!!!, Maggie screamed.

Maggie continued to pound the table with her fist. She shook her head as if she was trying to run away from something. Her eyes were full of fear and torment.

-- Daddy!!! Makaila!!!

Maggie grew silent. Father Ignacio's heart was pounding. His eyes welled up with tears. The fear and anguish he felt with Maggie's screaming he could no longer take. He began to pray for Maggie. Father Ignacio waited for Makaila to come out running with all the screaming and pounding Maggie was doing. But she didn't come out. Father Ignacio leaned in closer to Maggie and began to pray out loud. Maggie was still gone in her memory and Father Igancio worried that he wouldn't be able to get her out of there and back to this evening. Father Ignacio continued to call out for Maggie. Finally Maggie spoke.

-- He took me upstairs one day and made me sit on his lap on a rocking chair. Makaila was downstairs. "Oh God, no!! Stop it!! Stop!" Maggie began to scream again.

Father Ignacio started praying harder and louder, *"Dear Lord, Grant unto Maggie peace of mind.."* Maggie continued. She remembered running downstairs crying and screaming for Makaila. Makaila jumped up from the living room floor and called out for Maggie. Maggie was at the top of the stairs crying. Makaila asked what had happened. Mr. Brown came out behind Maggie trying to catch her and he was pretending to console Maggie, saying that she had stepped on a pin. Father Ignacio continued in his prayer and didn't skip a beat while Maggie was telling him this story. Just then Father Ignacio's head was filled with a vision. His lips went silent as his mind wandered. He could see Maggie in a basement, looking around when Maggie stumbled upon something on the floor. Maggie's mouth and eyes widened, her heart pounded in fear. She turned and ran up the stairs of the basement screaming and yelling. She couldn't get the door opened. She tried pulling and turning on the knob. The door did not move. She turned to look back down the stairs and screamed even louder. She tried desperately to get the door open, continuing to look back and turning to get the door open. Just then the door flew open and Maggie ran out and into an upstairs bedroom and hid in a closet. In the darkness of the closet, she slid down on the floor slowly and held her head. Her breaths came in frantic pants. Her tears sliding down her chin and dripping onto her legs that she had curled up underneath her. Her eyes fixed open. In the darkness of this closet, Maggie was never the same again.

Father Ignacio shook his head and threw himself back into his chair. His brow glistened with sweat, his breaths came fast as his heart eased its pounding. He closed his eyes and the vivid vision was still there. He quickly opened his eyes and noticied Maggie staring at him. Father Ignacio rubbed his hands together. Maggie finally spoke.

-- Father your hands! What did you do to your hands? Maggie frantically said.

Father Ignacio was trying to make out the words that were being said by Maggie. He didn't hear her. His hearing was muffled and every second that passed he felt the now burning sensation in his hands.

-- Father, what happened? Maggie said as she rose from her seat and grabbed a paper towel from the table.

Father Ignacio's hearing was getting better and he finally made out the words Maggie was saying. He looked down at his hands. His heart began to pound again. He lifted his hands in front of his face. His hands were bloody. He slowly turned each hand while he watched blood drip down his palms onto his wrist. Maggie quickly wrapped the paper towel on each hand. Father Ignacio's vision was blurred and he quite couldn't make out how he had cut his hands. His mind was cloudy. He blinked twice trying to regain his focus. Maggie wiped the blood from his hands and yelled out for Makaila.

-- Oh my God, what happened? Makaila said in a loud voice.

--I don't know. We were talking and by the time I knew it, I looked at Father Ignacio's hands and I noticied the blood. Maggie recited in a raised voice.

Both Makaila and Maggie wiped the blood off of Father Ignacio's hands and wrapped a clean paper towel over each one.

-- I'm alright. It's okay, really. Father Ignacio finally said. 'Look.... the bleeding stopped. I'll be okay."

Maggie looked at Father Ignacio's eyes and wondered what had happened and Maggie knew that Father didn't have a clue either. Makaila looked on the table and floor to find out how exactly Father Ignacio cut his hands. She didn't see anything out of the ordinary. Father Ignacio leaned back in his chair. The burning sensation he had felt in his hands had dissipated. He sat there quiet for a moment.

-- Maggie, are you alright, he asked.

-- Yes, I'm fine Father, Maggie answered.

Father Ignacio looked at his watch. The time was 10:22 PM. Father Ignacio realized that he wasn't feeling well. Something inside him stirred. He felt he needed to get home. He made some excuse about getting up early the next day. He asked for God's forgiveness in lying to Makaila and Maggie. He didn't want them to feel that they have been an imposition.

-- Are you really okay Maggie, he asked again.

-- Yes Father, I am fine.... don't worry.

-- Well, I must leave and let both of you get a good night's sleep. Sister Angelica is probably pacing the floor by now.

Makaila and Maggie both got up and showed Father Ignacio to the door. Father Ignacio picked up his coffee cup and saucer and Makaila insisted he leave it there on the table. He placed his hands in his pockets of his coat as they walked through the apartment. Upon reaching the door Father Ignacio turned around with a dismayed look on his face.

-- Let me ask you one last question, he said.

Both Maggie and Makaila nodded, as they noticied Father Ignacio in a tired state.

-- Did anyone else know what was happening at the Brown's house?

Makaila and Maggie looked at each other in unison.

-- No, not completely, Makaila answered.

-- I told a friend about the memories I was having and she told me that she had recalled going over to the Brown's house when she was younger to look through the basement windows.

-- And what did she see? Father Ignacio asked.

-- Nothing... the windows were blacked out with paint.

-- I asked dad just recently and he said that he just knew that we had changed at the age of seven and didn't know why, Makaila finished saying.

Makaila and Maggie got closer together. Their eyes had filled with tears. Father Ignacio hugged them both and continued out the door.

-- God bless, Father said as he headed for his car.

-- Good night Father, both Makaila and Maggie voiced out as they closed the door slowly.

Father Ignacio got into his car and fumbled for his keys in his pockets. He then realized that he was still wearing the make-shift bandages on his hands. He took a closer look at his hands and saw nothing. No cut, no scratch... only traces of dried blood where it was not wiped off completely. He prayed all the way home that night and for the next few days that followed.

Chapter Eleven

Father Ignacio

That evening was not a pleasant one for Father Ignacio. He felt terrible how he had just gotten up and left Makaila's apartment after the incident that night. He knew that he might have upset both Makaila and Maggie, probably thinking that it was too much for him. But they didn't realize that he was in for the long journey ahead of them. He would stay with them and never leave them. Father Ignacio knew that the one thing that both Makaila and Maggie needed was someone in their lives to believe them.... and he did.... probably more than they expected.

That night, Father Ignacio felt Maggie's pain and saw Maggie's memories. Father Ignacio was an instrument in seeing and hearing the past, the pain, the anguish, torment and the knowing.... and yet importantly, believing Maggie's and Makaila's story. Still, Father Ignacio felt badly about leaving shortly after the incident. He clearly knew that Maggie had gone to the Brown's house in her mind and wouldn't have probably been able to get out. It was then that Father Ignacio had gone in after her. Something or someone was trying to keep her there.

Much unexplained factors of his recollection about his hands that night seemed to drift further away into his subconscience. He felt that as important and weird that he had cut his hand on something and with no proof of having a puncture wound or scar, it had seemed almost miraculous. He questioned if even he was the one who was bleeding. The more he thought about that moment, the more unclear his thoughts were and the less sense the whole thing made.

Father Ignacio played his head like a recorder that he would rewind and stop and rewind and play back again. He recollected Maggie's words, actions and physical attributes. Father Ignacio felt lost for Maggie knowing that a whole, horrid past life-experience was buried somewhere in her being and knowing this he worried about the day that those memories would unleash a torrent of deceit, anguish, and betrayal. He worried for both of them..... and he worried that both Makaila and Maggie didn't have a clue about what was to unfold in their lives.

As he thought, Sister Angelica was pacing the floor that evening when he finally showed up at 11:30. And much to his surprise, she didn't say a word apart from her relieved-look on her face.

~ ~ ~

They watched Father Ignacio walk to his car that was parked in front of Makaila's apartment. They smiled when they heard Father say "God bless" to them. Makaila slowly closed the door. Inside the apartment Maggie slumped down on the couch and Makaila locked the door. Outside they heard the soft, solid "thud" the car door made when Father Ignacio closed it. They waited for the sound of the engine start up and it didn't happen as quickly as they thought it would. Finally, they heard the engine crank over after a couple of minutes and saw the headlights of his car shine through the window and blinds of her apartment. Makaila sat next to Maggie who was rubbing her temples.

-- What the heck was that about? Maggie finally spoke softly.

Makaila just shrugged her shoulders.

-- That was so damn weird. How did he cut himself? she continued.

-- What were you guys doing when that happened? Makaila asked ever so slowly, almost afraid to hear the answer.

-- Nothing, absolutely nothing... Maggie said with a shocked look on her face.

-- Nothing? Makaila questioned.

-- We were just talking, and then, I don't know what happened. I was trying to remember something and then I heard Father Ignacio scream out something in Spanish, I think it was Spanish.... and then I saw the blood on his hands.

-- I couldn't find anything that he could have cut his hands on when I looked earlier, Makaila said.

They sat there in silence for a few minutes. Maggie kicked off her shoes and pulled her legs up on the couch. She tried to remember exactly what they were talking about and for the life of her, it seemed that it was all a fog.

-- Makaila, do you think we freaked him out?

-- No, I think he was very tired tonight, and I am sure he didn't want to be an imposition any longer than he thought he was.

-- Do you think he'll call or come back? Maggie asked almost sheepishly.

-- Of course he will, Makaila quickly answered. He is such a good man, and he is the only one who has ever completely and unconditionally believed us. He won't abandon us. I know he won't.

-- I guess you're right, Makaila..... You're right, but I don't know, I feel that he will let us go one day but I think that we'll be all right, we'll be okay. Maggie said as she closed her eyes.

Makaila looked down at Maggie. She smiled and thought, "we both were each other's strength and each other's hope, nothing can ever separate us.... nothing."

~ ~ ~

Father Ignacio woke up the next morning, feeling like he was hit by a runaway train. He could smell breakfast cooking on the kitchen stove. No doubt that Sister Angelica was "up and at em'" at the crack of dawn. Father Ignacio marveled at Sister's strength. He knew that she did not get to sleep until late and here she was cooking up one of her famous "Mexican breakfasts." Traces of memory from last night at Makaila's jumped around in his head. He clearly remembered what had happened and he clearly and vividly recalled the vision he experienced. To him, it happened and to him he was there in the basement with Maggie. Father Ignacio laid on his bed. He turned his head to one side and noticed the brilliance of light the sunshine made seeping through his window. He smiled and thanked God. He stretched his arms over his head and yawned, breathing in life of a new day. He brought his hands down and looked at them. He studied them, he turned them from side to side, palm side up and palm side down. He brought his hands together as in prayer and brought them to his lips. He closed his eyes and recited his morning prayers, thanking God for all his blessings, his mistakes and his forthcomings..... and for life.

Father Ignacio thanked Sister Angelica for a wonderful breakfast as he rubbed his stomach in response of being asked if he wanted more. Father Ignacio retired to his bedroom since he had a few minutes before morning Mass started. He gathered his notes and things and headed out the door only to notice the makeshift bandages on the floor by his bed from the night before. He picked them up and tossed them in the wastebasket nearby. He looked at his hands again and slowly walked out the door with a perplexed look on his face.

~ ~ ~

Celebrating Mass has always been an exceptional blessing for him. He reminisces about his altar boy days alongside Monsignor Kealy. While listening to the Liturgy of the Word, he asked for God's forgiveness, when his mind wandered to the episodes of last night. He tried to focus on the Word as it was being proclaimed and his reading of the Gospel cleared his head a little. He gave his Homily with a warm reception from the parishioners who gently nodded their heads in agreement to his words. While he sat contemplating on the Gospel just read and of his Homily, his mind wandered elsewhere.

The most important part of the Mass was at hand, The Consecration of the Eucharist. Father Ignacio stood at the altar with his white alb that extended down to his hands and whenever he outstretched his arms the children always thought that he had sprouted wings. His green stole worn around his neck that laced down both sides of his body and down the length of his robe looked brilliantly in place. He felt special and blessed by his participation in bringing a community of believers together in celebration and in worship of God.

With his outstretched arms Father Ignacio recited out of the Sacramentary. *"On the night He was betrayed, He took bread, He broke the bread, gave it to His disciples and said, "take this all of you and eat it, this is my body, which will be given up for you....."* He brought his arms down and laid his hands over the communion host and he continued to recite....*"do this, in memory of me..."* and he bowed his head and genuflected in honor. Just then a flash of light burst into his mind. He saw Maggie climbing up the steps of the basement, running and tripping over the steps as she made her way to the top of the stairs. Her face looked frightened as she screamed at whatever she saw behind her.... another flash of light burst in his mind and the vision was over. Father Ignacio stood back up from behind the altar. He looked out into the congregation, nobody had seemed to notice anything out of the ordinary. He cleared his throat and continued in the Consecration rite; *"take this all of you and drink from it. This is the cup of my blood, the blood of the new and everlasting covenant, it shall be shed for you and for all, so that sins may be forgiven, "* Father Ignacio laid his hands over the Chalice... *"do this in memory of me."* He bowed and genuflected. Another burst of light entered his mind... he saw Maggie at the top of the stairs trying desperately to get the door open. She continued to look back... her eyes widened, tears rolled down her cheek. She screamed and yelled for Makaila and her father.... she tore at the doorknob, using all her might to turn it. Maggie's screams echoed in Father Ignacio's ears. The vision panned down the stairs.... the darkness seemed to creep slowly up the stairs. Father Ignacio could hear the sounds of footsteps getting louder and louder. Out farther back in the darkness, he could see flickering lights and hear sinister sounds emanating from the dark form below. Maggie's screams became louder and louder.... her heart pounded out of her chest, tears flowed down her chin, her eyes were wide and full of fear. She grew tired and exhaustion filled her body. Her legs almost collapsed underneath her, but she tried so hard to get out. Father

Ignacio's vision panned around the darkening room of the basement. He saw vague outlines of what seemed to be figures and a row of flickering lights outlined a circle... His vision continued back up the stairs to Maggie. The sounds were getting louder and the footsteps were getting closer.... and at the bottom of the stairs Father Ignacio saw himself!

In his vision, he saw himself hold up a book in both of his hands out in front of him as if trying to keep back whatever wanted to get closer to Maggie. Father Ignacio held on tight. Sweat poured from his forehead and down his face. His hair tasselled from side to side every time he looked back at Maggie and back down at the darkness. He inched his way up the stairs one step at a time. His feet stumbled against a step as he stepped backwards. He held tight to the book now glowing in his hands. It trembled under Father Ignacio's strength and shook like it wanted to fly out of his hand. It burned and glowed in power, fighting off and warding off the evil from getting closer to Maggie. Father Ignacio held strong to his position. He prayed loud and yelled at Maggie, "Maggie, get yourself out! You can get yourself out! Only you can do it." Only Maggie did not see or hear Father Ignacio's words. To Maggie, she was the only one down there, trying to free herself and she really didn't think that she would make it out alive. "Maggie!!! Get out!" Father Ignacio yelled. The darkness crept up closer to the bottom steps.... the book in his hands shook with a mighty force... it trembled, glowed and bright lights escaped from it's pages within, creating streams of light against the walls.... A flash of light and Father Ignacio fell backwards on the steps, "Maggie run!" Maggie screamed at the top of her lungs and the door she so desperately tried to open, burst open.... the door knob fell to the ground near Father Ignacio. He reached for it with one hand, still holding tight to the book close to his chest. As he picked up the doorknob, it slipped out of his hand and bounced down the remaining steps.

The doorknob rested on the bottom step glistening with Maggie's tears and sweat and Father Ignacio's blood that was left there from his hand ..... he brought his hand up to his face. His hand was blistered and he felt the burning pains..... he closed his eyes.

Father Ignacio opened up his eyes. The congregation was now slowly standing up from kneeling and the low hum of unison prayer echoed in the church. Father Ignacio looked from one side of the church to the other, down the middle aisle and from one side of the sanctuary to the other. Everyone continued in their prayer and Father Ignacio slowly began to mouth the same prayer. Nobody seemed to have noticed a thing and the remaining Mass went on as usual. Father Ignacio remembered clearly the vision before him and what seemed like an eternity of minutes were only a few microseconds. The only traces were that of the vision and the now burning sensation in his hands.

~ ~ ~

A week had gone by since the vision that one particular Sunday and from the time that Father Ignacio had spoken with Makaila and Maggie. He had taken the week off. He was uncertain of what and how he was feeling. He felt tired and drained and his energy had escaped him. Sister Angelica nursed him to health as she has done in the past not realizing that Father Ignacio was not suffering from the common flu, but nonetheless, it helped him. He slept in plenty and when he wasn't resting, he was praying. Friday morning he picked up the telephone to call Makaila. His hands were still a little sore and a little pain was noticeable. Makaila answered;

-- Makaila, this is Father Ignacio.

-- Father, oh, Father, how are you?

-- I am well Makaila. How are you and Maggie?

-- We are so good Father. Maggie will be thrilled that you have called.

-- Is she there, I would love to say hello to her.

-- I am so sorry Father. She had to leave for home earlier than planned.

-- I am so sorry to hear that, Makaila. I'm sure you are disappointed that her trip was cut short.

-- Oh, I am fine Father. We made plans to get together soon. She promised me.

-- That's very good Makaila. I wanted to apologize for not calling sooner.

-- Father please, you have been such a big help already. There is nothing to apologize for. Maggie left here almost a new person. I haven't seen her this free for a long time. Father, I don't know what you did or what you said to her that night, but she is a changed person. Thank you so much, Father, thank you.

-- Its been my pleasure and honor to be able to help in anyway I can.

Father Ignacio said this trying to hold back the tears that welled up in his eyes. He was afraid that his voice would crack with the lump he had in his throat, so he cut his conversation with Makaila short with promises of getting together upon his arrival.

-- I will be in touch Makaila, Father Ignacio promised her. And Makaila?......
know that you can call on me anytime.

-- Father thank you so much. I don't know how to thank you, Makaila said with
obvious sounds of a sweet cry of gratefulness.

-- Just continue to have faith Makaila, that's all the thanks I need.

And with that, Father Ignacio hung up the receiver. His eyes welled up with
tears as he marveled at the victory God was glorious on. Somehow Maggie was
in a different state than she was when she first met her..... And Makaila seemed
joyously happy. Father Ignacio was going to miss Makaila; and Makaila made
it clear to Father Ignacio that she was to miss him. Father Ignacio told Makaila
that he would be taking a three-month vacation to Mexico as his help was
needed there as requested of him by the Bishop. Father Ignacio took this as a
sabbatical and as much as he hated leaving his parish, he felt it the best thing
for him.

Father Ignacio's trip to Mexico was scheduled for the upcoming Monday and
Father Ignacio had one last Sunday before he left to celebrate Mass. Sister
Angelica had hugged him and cried over him several times a day as soon as she
heard the news that Father Ignacio was leaving and celebrating Mass with him
on that last Sunday was going to be a difficult one. Father Ignacio was touched
by the reception he was given by the parishioners and his only thought was if
he was going to experience what he had experienced through vision the week
prior. But to his relief, the vision did not return.

That evening, Father Ignacio was packing his bags in his room. Sister Angelica had just left after coming in and hugging him and finishing off a box of Kleenix she had just opened that morning, when the phone rang. It was Makaila.

-- Father, I have someone here on the other line, who wants to say hello.

-- Father Ignacio, it's Maggie. I just wanted to tell you to be safe out there and to tell you "thank you," for everything.

-- Maggie?? Are you in town?

-- No Father, Makaila chirped in. I have her on three-way.

-- Oh,.... well, thank you Maggie. It was indeed my pleasure. When will you be back ? he continued.

-- Soon Father, very soon I hope, Maggie answered.

-- Well then, thank you for calling. I will look forward to seeing your faces again soon. God bless and do take care of yourselves.

-- Father, we will, oh and Father, we've couldn't have done it without you, were Makaila's final words.

-- Good night and may God always keep you in his hands, Father Ignacio said as he slid the telephone off his ear.

He paused there for a moment. Smiling. His heart so full of joy and a sense of victory overshadowed him. He looked up into heaven from his window in his room and said, "I couldn't have done it without you... thank you Lord." He slowly put the phone down on the receiver and closed his eyes and prayed.

~ ~ ~

Father Ignacio wasn't gone for more than a week when Sister Angelica picked up her telephone and dialed Monsignor Kealy's number. They spoke briefly.

-- Yes Monsignor, he has left already. He called me yesterday to tell me that he got into Mexico okay...No, I haven't checked yet. What exactly does it look like? ...I am so worried about him... Yes, Monsignor, if and when I find it I will call you...Yes, I knew that this day would come. I just didn't expect it this soon... I will, yes...God bless you Monsignor...Good-bye.

~ ~ ~

A couple of months had gone by and Makaila was on her way to visit Maggie. Even though on the outside she was jumping for joy and excited about seeing her, her insides were a little more frazzled and unclear. A certain development would occur in both of their lives and they quite weren't sure what it was going to be. Makaila missed Father Ignacio and now she felt that she needed to at least talk to him. Makaila hadn't been sleeping well and she felt that her defenses were on guard all the time. She prayed a lot and would often catch herself praying out loud. Both Makaila and Maggie have been so complete since that last night they saw Father Ignacio. Now, Makaila went through her days with strange thoughts and pictures that circled her head. Often times she would just shrug them off as if they were passing thoughts. But the more time that passed the harder it was to dismiss them and little did Makaila know that Maggie was experiencing the same thing.... even worse.

A few days into her visit with Maggie, Makaila felt as though she was on pins and needles and they both seemed to be on the edge with each other. Makaila and Maggie felt that something was trying to tear them apart and come between them. Both Makaila and Maggie felt this familiar sense.

One day in her visit, Maggie was soaking in the bathtub while Makaila pulled up a chair next to her. Maggie was silent. Makaila noticed that Maggie wanted to say something and she noticed how much trouble she was having getting the words out. Makaila started talking about life and its troubles and its rewards, just like they always have done. Maggie broke the conversation.

-- Makaila, there is something I have to tell you...

-- What about? Makaila asked.

Makaila was looking down at her hands as she was filing them with an emery board. She did not expect the words that came out of Maggie's mouth.

-- I'm having memories. Maggie continued.

Makaila continued filing her fingernails. She felt at ease until Maggie said the words that sent Makaila into a traumatic panic.

-- I'm having memories of people in dark robes walking in a circle in the Browns basement.

Makaila felt terror run through her body. She dropped the emery board. She stood up and started screaming. She could barely hear Maggie calling her through her blood curdling screams and it seemed that a steel door had gone up in her head and a flood of visual memories she had never had before came rushing through. Makaila was screaming out of control.

-- Oh my God, Oh my God!!, Makaila yelled through her screams.

-- Do you remember anything? Maggie asked her.

-- I don't, I just remember them carrying candles.... Oh God!! Oh God!!, Makaila continued.

-- Do you remember anything else? Maggie asked.

Makaila's head swam with the unleashing of memories and the vivid pictures she saw. Makaila remembered the basement of the Browns. There was a table in the middle of the floor, a candelabra and the direction the people were coming from. Makaila felt frozen inside, not being able to run but so wanting to do so. Makaila could barely take in when Maggie said that she remembered that too and just wanted to know if she remembered the same thing.

They were connected. Their darkest memories were finally something they could remember together.

Makaila felt completely in a daze the rest of her visit with Maggie. They held onto each other even more than they had done in the past. It was a couple of days later after Makaila returned back to her home that Maggie called. Their memories were so identical and they trained each other not to coax or influence the other when they each had a memory. They decided to write them down on a list and later compare them. Their memories kept flashing through their heads. It was incredible how their memories surfaced at the same time. They learned to say to each other, "I've had memories, have you?" and it was only their trust in God who lifted them each time they did this and their motive was to heal from it all.

After those initial memories, Makaila was the one who carried on their motive. Maggie was shutting down. Makaila felt that Maggie saved her by the unleashing of memories and Makaila now felt that she needed to save Maggie from the basement and the rest of the Browns house.

-- You have to keep talking about this, Makaila would say to Maggie. It's the only way we won't be trapped in the basement anymore.

Makaila felt that she wouldn't be able to heal completely without knowing that Maggie wasn't running up those steps with her. She knew she wasn't frozen anymore and Makaila owed it to Maggie. Makaila felt that Maggie was the one who remembered for her and the one who was going to put a stop to the memories. Makaila figured out that the memories of the Browns basement were her subconscience memories and the upstairs were her conscience ones. It was a freedom she hadn't felt in a long time and now she needed to help Maggie. Makaila was so glad that they were together in their memories, but had no idea what was to come. Maggie called Makaila on the third day after the memories and after idle chitchat, Maggie remarked on something.

-- Makaila.... Maggie said.

-- Yeah... Makaila responded.

-- I have to tell you something else......

Makaila tensed up. She stopped breathing for a moment. Her reactions were ready to hear something worse than what had happened at Maggie's.

-- I remember mom being there.... Maggie said softly.

The kitchen counter Makaila was leaning on was the only thing holding her up. Makaila's eyes widened, her heart began to pound; that was the one memory she so wanted to be different than Maggie's. Makaila struggled with that memory because it was the identical memory she was having and it was the one that she wanted to be wrong about.

~ ~ ~

And in Mexico, Father Ignacio stirred in his sleep.... and his hands began to have that burning sensation again.

Chapter Twelve

Lalee's and Jack's Visit

A couple of weeks have gone by and both Makaila and Maggie struggled with their identical memories. Makaila so desperately wanted not to believe the memory of her mother being involved; but the more she denied it the clearer the memories were. Both Makaila's and Maggie's memories were identical whenever they compared their lists and this in itself made them feel abandoned. Their thoughts through this whole thing were that it was true. Their memories justified their lives. Makaila was putting the pieces together. She figured out the reason why she was so frozen when she went in to any basement, why she felt like she could just scream and run out of control and why her body raced inside. Both of their memories of the Browns basement became clearer as each day passed.

Makaila remembered hiding against a wall and under the stairs of the basement. She could see people dressed in dark robes, walking single file and carrying candles. And the worst of her memory was that of seeing her mother as clear as day among them and the confusing thing was that Makaila only embarked on how beautiful her mother still was. Makaila could remember weird sounds and evil laughter. She remembered blood and animals being killed with an ax of some sort. The memory alone sent Makaila's body into fright. Other pieces of memory flashed through her mind. She had visions of baby chickens being there one day and gone the next and her mind saw people being hung by their hands. Makaila also realized that the dreams she was having throughout her life made a lot of sense now. She often dreamed about being trapped in a dark house and she was determined to find the way out for her and Maggie. She desperately wanted to get to the light at the door at the top of the stairs that led outside to freedom and to God.

After Makaila and Maggie were convinced that their mother was involved, Maggie starting shutting down even more. She no longer wanted to deal with the lists of memories and it was Makaila who pushed it and insisted. Makaila felt that she needed to help Maggie with her conscious memories as Maggie helped Makaila with her unconscious ones... and Makaila was not going to abandon Maggie... she was not going to leave Maggie in the basement... she was not going to let the Browns take her... Makaila wanted to see the two of them climb up those steps "together," open up the door "together" and feel the warmth of the bright light..."together."

Throughout their lives growing up, Makaila insisted that they not talk about the Browns. This rule was applied even to their mother Lalee who over the years still had some sort of contact with them. Makaila now thought about how weird and strange it was that the Browns would always pop in and out of their lives. Just when the twins thought that they had gotten rid of the Browns by moving across town or by changing schools, they would always seem to follow. Both Makaila and Maggie remarked how strange it was that when they moved far across the city where they lived, Mrs. Brown would show up as their Home Economics teacher or when they came home one day and found Mrs. Brown talking to their mother visible through the window of their house. Every single time they thought they would not see the Browns anymore, they skipped along the sidewalk, but the Brown's would show up, no matter how far or how many years have gone by and the twins felt like they couldn't skip anymore.

~ ~ ~

Jack and Lalee came to visit Makaila. Makaila saw for the first time how old they were getting. Makaila saw her mother through different eyes this time and part of her heart ached for the betrayal her mother had caused and at the same time for pity. Lalee was no longer the beautiful classy woman she used to be. Her drinking and addiction to medication had taken most of her body, and her face told a thousand tales of troubles and held back a thousand lies and secrets. It was this particular visit that Makaila was going to get some answers of some sort. Makaila's strategy was to bring the Browns up in conversation even though their name was not to be mentioned before; a rule set forth by Makaila herself years ago.

When Makaila asked questions about the Browns, Lalee scrambled in her chair and she was agitated that she could not sit still. Yet, the answers that Makaila wanted were not surfacing. Makaila did notice her mother's uneasiness and her agitation whenever the Browns were brought up in conversation. Makaila also noticed that her father did not like the Browns as that was obvious as he did not want to participate in conversations regarding them.

During that time, Makaila and her mother and father took a day trip as part of their sight-seeing visit. When Makaila's father fell asleep in the back seat of her car, Lalee brought up the Browns.

-- Bonnie has been deathly sick, Lalee said.

And very cleverly and coy, she continued saying....

-- What do you remember about them?

Lalee squirmed in her seat and Makaila's heart jumped.

-- What do "you" remember Mom? Makaila asked empowered-like.

Lalee stared out the window. She turned around and answered Makaila.

-- I didn't make you go to Florida with them because I was afraid they would drown you in the ocean.

Makaila's heart stopped. A fear rippled up and down her spine. How she didn't swerve the car out of control was beyond her comprehension. Makaila did not expect her to say what she just heard. Makaila and Lalee sat quietly for a long time and Makaila was in awe. The Browns often mentioned taking Makaila to Florida with them and Makaila felt fear every time they talked about it. Bonnie often told Makaila that they would drown her in the ocean and Makaila never told a living soul about her fear.

The rest of their visit, not one word was mentioned about what Lalee told Makaila. The Browns' were not brought up again and before Makaila knew it, they were gone. Makaila talked with Maggie about it and they both held onto each other. Maggie was shutting down even more and Makaila knew that Maggie was stuck between the present and the Browns' basement.... and Makaila was not going to leave her there.

~ ~ ~

When Makaila was lecturing a group of abused women shortly after her parents visit, right in the middle of her lecture Makaila felt like she was shutting down.

The words of her mother played and rang out in her head, *'I tried getting rid of you as kids and it didn't work."* Makaila felt professionally embarrassed and she was determined to do something about it. She went home that evening and made a plane reservation to where her parents lived, she wanted more answers and she wanted Lalee to tell her the truth about what went on at the Browns' basement.

A day later, Makaila's father called.

-- Makaila, why are you coming? Jack said in his stern voice.

-- To confront mom about the Browns, Makaila answered.

Jack continued in his authoritative voice.

-- What's your motive?

-- To free Maggie from this bondage, Makaila said with conviction in her voice.

-- You know I could refuse you in coming?

-- Yes, I know, Makaila said out of respect.

The phone was silent for a second. Makaila thought about how serious her dad was when he said that he could refuse her from coming. Finally Jack's voice came through the phone. This time his voice was not so stern.

-- You can come and do this.... but I will not be in the room when you do, Jack said calmly. " I believe and trust you," he added.

-- Dad are you gonna be okay? Makiala asked.

-- I'll handle this like I have handled everything else. I'll be fine, Jack answered.

Makaila was sad for her father as she slowly hung up the telephone.

~ ~ ~

Makaila went spiritually prepared and knew she wanted to confront her mother on Sunday. When she was there, she found a book of prayers amongst other books on their shelf. Makaila went into the bathroom Sunday morning where it was private, and recited the prayer she had found. Makaila asked for strength, she asked for courage and she asked for peace out of this whole thing. She asked for Father Ignacio to hear her and pray for her as well. The time had come.

Makaila walked into the kitchen and motioned to her dad that this was it. Jack left the room as if he had work to do out in his garden. Makaila sat next to her mom at the kitchen counter.

-- Mom, I have to tell you something, Makaila said still feeling strong.

Lalee grabbed Makaila's hand and squeezed it;

-- Oh baby, what is it? Lalee answered.

Makaila never once remembered when her mother called her "baby" and before Makaila could answer, Lalee continued.

-- There are two things I could not live through, she said as she hung her head as in shame, "One, if you and Maggie didn't love me anymore... and two, If I had to go back to a mental hospital"

Makaila reassured her with compassion that would never happen, and without a beat, Makaila continued on her reason for being there.

-- Mom, I remember you in a dark robe, carrying a candle, walking with others in the Brown's basement.......

Lalee had the most astonished look on her face. Makaila studied her every action. Lalee looked up to the ceiling....

-- Oh, my God!... oh, my God!!... oh my God!!!... Lalee said with a different emphasis each time knowing that the truth had surfaced... "Oh my God!... oh my God!!..."

Makaila was astonished on how, within a blink of eye, Lalee looked at her cold as ice and said; *"I don't remember..."* Makaila just sat there trying to figure her out her mother's game. Makaila was convinced that she knew what she was talking about. Her mother reverted back to the helpless victim she always was.

-- But I will help you with what you remember, Lalee finally offered.

Makaila didn't realize it at the time and it took her awhile to sense what had just happened. The truth of the matter was that Lalee did not deny it and Makaila wasn't sure what to make of it.

-- What do you want me to do? Lalee asked Makaila.

-- Help Maggie.... she is very lost, Makaila answered.

Makaila called Maggie and told her what happened. Lalee just sat there on that bar stool smoking a cigarette, shaking. Makaila handed her mother the phone.

-- How can I help you Maggie? Lalee asked endearingly.

Maggie talked to Lalee for a few seconds and mentioned something that Bonnie had done. Lalee's attitude and demeanor changed and in an evil tone of voice said; "That's a black lie!" Both Makaila and Maggie did not know what to do with what and how she said that. Part of Makaila believed that she didn't remember, but the other part of Makaila knew for certain that she was there.

At that time, Makaila thought it was over... that they were on their way to healing.... but Maggie.... Maggie didn't believe her mother..... and little did Makaila know that Maggie was right.

After some more talking, Lalee felt remorse for what the girls had remembered. And Makaila felt that she had done her part in getting the initial truth out. Makaila dropped it after a while and she and Lalee bonded that day like they had done years ago when Makaila was a child. They played the piano together and they both smiled inside and appreciated the new found bond they were experiencing. Makaila felt that since the truth was out and Lalee was willing to help sort out the pieces that their lives could go on and make up for lost time. Makaila felt that her mother was truly sorry and at the end of Makaila's visit, they hugged in hopes that the process of love and peace will begin and that Lalee would feel better about herself instead of sabotaging her life. Makaila just prayed that Maggie would get to this place soon.

~ ~ ~

Father Ignacio for the past week had been feeling quite homesick and the thought that he would be returning to his parish in less than a month seemed to keep him going. He had written to Monsignor Kealy and to Sister Angelica over the last few weeks. He wrote to Makaila early in his arrival to Mexico but not since then. Father Ignacio had lately been thinking of Makaila and Maggie, praying and hoping that they have continued in their new found peace. But he had them on his mind lately, more than usual, and he thought it just to be homesick for Sister's scolding and the usual parish demands.

Father Ignacio tossed and turned in bed one night while he lay sleeping. His head cocked from one side to the other... sweat glistened off his forehead. Father Ignacio awoke and bolted straight up in his bed.

-- Oh dear God, Oh dear God, he whispered.

It was then that Father Ignacio finally realized that Makaila and Maggie, and as hard as it was for him to believe it, had been exposed to the occult. An occult where people worshipped Satan, where evil played on young and vulnerable minds...... where the Browns wanted to sacrifice either one or both of them. Father Ignacio, in his vision, saw people being hung by their hands and animals being sacrificed for their blood. Father Ignacio was convinced that the true and pure innocence of Makaila and Maggie was going to be the Browns ultimate sacrifice to their demons, and ultimately to the prince of darkness for power, greed and belief. Father Ignacio crossed himself and began to pray to the ultimate God, the Father Almighty, the giver of life..... he prayed to his heavenly Father to remove the replaying thoughts out of his head, he prayed hard for Makaila and Maggie requesting that an army of angels be at their side always.

~ ~ ~

Father Ignacio couldn't get home fast enough. His last four weeks in Mexico seemed to drag by ever so slowly. Seeing Sister Angelica at the top of the airline walkway made his heart pound out of excitement. *"I am home"*, he whispered. *"I am home."*

On the ride to the rectory, Sister Angelica talked nonstop not letting Father get in a word. She went on and on about how horrible the replacement priest was and the congregation was ready to walk out and picket in front of the church. She went on to describe her meetings and accomplishments, the daily hustle-bustle of running a parish, how she ran out of candles and how the youth group decided to make a mess in the auditorium during one of their rallys. Father Ignacio just listened, nodded his head and smiled. *"Ah yes, I am home...."* When Sister Angelica paused for a second to catch her breath, he asked if Makaila or Maggie had ever called in the time he was gone.

-- No, no.... did you not tell them that you were going out of the country, Father? Sister Angelica asked.

-- I was just curious if they had called that's all, Father Ignacio retorted back. "And did Monsignor Kealy call while I was away?" he continued to ask.

Sister Angelica grew silent for a second.

-- No, I don't think he did.

Sister Angelica slumped into her seat and Father watched her lips as she said something under her breath.

-- I must call him, when I get in to the rectory, Father Ignacio stated.

-- Yes, yes, you must, Sister Angelica finally said.

And with that, Sister Angelica started up again. She talked about the gardener, the Altar Boys, the ladie's groups and that the Diocese was getting on her nerves. Father Ignacio laughed inside and shook his head as they drove home.

~ ~ ~

At the rectory Father Ignacio headed straight to his bedroom to unpack while Sister Angelica insisted she make him something to eat. Father Ignacio opened up his door to his bedroom and a warm feeling of home overcame him. He plopped his suitcase on the bed and took off his coat and hung it on the hook near his door. He opened his suitcase and began removing its contents and placing them properly in their prospective places. He pulled out a couple of boxes of gifts he had brought back for Sister Angelica and two small boxes he brought back for Makaila and Maggie. Father Ignacio sat at the edge of his bed

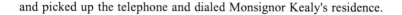

and picked up the telephone and dialed Monsignor Kealy's residence.

-- Hello?

-- Monsignor Kealy? It's Ignacio.

-- Who is this? Monsignor Kealy screamed.

-- It's me, Monsignor, Ignacio, he said in a louder voice.

-- Nachito my boy, How are you? Are you back home? Monsignor finally answered as he finally heard who it was.

-- Yes, I am home now and I am fine... How are you Monsignor?

-- Well, I would be better if you came to visit, Monsignor Kealy added.

Father Ignacio smiled as he had to yell into the phone in order for Monsignor Kealy to hear him. He made plans to visit home soon. Monsignor Kealy was excited at that.

-- How are you really doing my boy? Monsignor Kealy asked somberly.

-- I feel great, Monsignor, never better....ready to do some new work here in the parish. I want to share with you some ideas I have, he said excitedly.

Father Ignacio continued talking with Monsignor Kealy while he finished unpacking. He grabbed the contents of his briefcase and headed for his closet.

He pulled out the safe that sat in the corner and opened it. He moved things around and removed things from inside of it as if making room for other things he had to put in there. He laid some things on the floor and the book he placed in there months ago was accidently left out on the floor while he locked up the safe.

Father Ignacio just had finished unpacking and saying good-bye to Monsignor Kealy when Sister Angelica's voice echoed through the rectory.

-- Father Ignacio? Father Ignacio? Come and eat... it'll get cold!

Father Ignacio smiled and shook his head and was so happy to be home again.

After dinner, Father Ignacio insisted that he take a walk around the church grounds. On his walk, he admired the church's architecture in front of the now glowing sunset in the background. He noticed the freshly planted flowers and shrubs along the sidewalk of the church. He passed by a door and out of habit he pulled on it making certain that it was locked. He peered in a window at the vestibule of the church and noticed the Sanctuary lamp burning as always, glowing in the dimly lit church. He signed himself and gently bowed in the direction of the Tabernacle. He thanked God for a safe journey, a happy return, Sister Angelica's cooking and Monsignor Kealy's love...... and the beautiful sunset that felt like it was especially painted tonight by God's hands for Father Ignacio.

In the rectory, Sister Angelica hummed loudly one of her favorite hymns while finishing off the dishes and strolling around picking up things that needed picking up. She found herself down the hall from Father Ignacio's bedroom. On the floor, there was something that seemed what looked like a wrapper or note of some kind. Sister continued humming while bending over to pick it up, and as she suspected, it was something for the trash can. Father Ignacio's door was open, and Sister Angelica peeked in. She walked in and quickly walked out as she heard Father Ignacio open the front door of the rectory.

-- I was getting worried, Father. Sister Angelica scolded.

-- Oh, Sister... I was just patrolling the church grounds. I am so happy to be home, he said.

-- and I am happy you are home too, Sister Angelica added.

Father Ignacio went to bed that night feeling so humbly blessed to be back home and in his own bed. He thought of that night in Mexico where he woke up from a disturbing dream about the reality of Makaila's and Maggie's life experience. He thought how genuine God was to hide those memories from them until they were able to handle it and deal with their reality. How does a person at an early age, cope with the fact that they were exposed to a cult where evil, hatred, betrayal, deceit, torture, torment and anguish were their belief system? And a belief where they stood against everything that's good, against God, Jesus, and the Holy Spirit. Father Ignacio thanked God for protecting them as they grew up to be the women they were today. He marveled at the thought on how Makaila and Maggie survived through all this and he felt in his heart and in faith that their spirits in them kept them safe, strong and kept their souls pure. But the hardest part was yet to come for Father Ignacio. How was he to tell that both Makaila and Maggie were exposed to a religion which they worshipped the Anti-Christ, the devil, an unpure religion? Father Ignacio had to think on how to handle it delicately and he was having a hard time trying to figure that out. Father Ignacio felt that maybe the truth didn't need to be told to them. Maybe the experiences they have already gone through and the releasing of those memories in their talks would be all that they would need. There would be no need possibly to even tell them. Maybe what they had already gone through was all there was and it satisfied their souls. Maybe they could live as they were meant to live; clean, pure of heart, happy, loved, peaceful and full of the Lord's blessings. *"Maybe,"* Father Ignacio thought to himself, *"maybe I don't need to say anymore...."* and with that, Father Ignacio drifted off to a peaceful sleep.

Father Ignacio felt content that there was a possibility that he didn't need to say any more to Makaila and Maggie. But, unbeknownst to him, the memories had gotten worse. Maggie was slipping further back and Makaila was growing tired. Father Ignacio was going to hear that their mother, the person who brought them into this world, was involved with the Browns in a way that was almost unforgiving by God. That she was part of the plot to do harm to two innocent, special unique gifts from heaven that God had entrusted her with? Father Ignacio was unaware of the depth Lalee was involved. He was unaware that the hardest memories had surfaced while he was away. That Makaila was going to be an instrument in their victory.... And that Maggie would have an important role in the process of this story unraveling now; and the events, rather difficult and painful, would finally be victorious over what the devil wanted to destroy. They all three didn't have a clue, and in heaven, God sent more blessings their way and thoughts of trust and faith grew stronger in them.

~ ~ ~

In her bedroom, Makaila laid awake in bed. Thoughts of the past week and Maggie's unexpected surgery had her concerned for her. She felt very uncomfortable. Maggie had just come out of surgery and it killed Makaila that she wasn't there to support her. What occupied her mind the most was the incident that happened with Maggie after coming home from the hospital and Lalee and Jack went to visit her. Makaila desperately tried to put the pieces together and she didn't know that some of the pieces had not surfaced yet. Maggie called her that evening and told what happened.

~ ~ ~

Maggie was laying in bed. She had been on pain medication for surgery and was on pain medication when she was sent home. Her parents wanted to come and see Maggie and Maggie thought it strange, since they had never been there for her before during one of her other surgeries. Maggie was half asleep and half under the effects of the medication when Lalee entered her room. Lalee was drunk, had a cigarette in one hand and a drink in the other. Maggie slowly opened her eyes and tried to focus on who was standing by her bed. She was completely groggy and almost incoherent but there was no mistake about what happened. There was evil in her mom's voice....

-- so, what "do you" remember about the Browns? Lalee said in her drunken stupor.

Maggie composed herself a little and a clear mind followed after what she heard her mother ask her.

-- *"I don't want to talk about it,'* was all that Maggie could say and Lalee turned and walked out the door.

Makaila lay in bed as tears rolled down her face onto her pillow. Makaila thought that this story was over and now felt that it was far from being over. She needed to help, support and guide Maggie. Maggie was still stuck in the Browns basement for some reason and there was no way that Makaila would let her stay there. Maggie was still down there for a purpose and Makaila had faith that the day would come when they would be able to again skip down the sidewalk together, hand in hand as little girls...... before that portion of their life was stolen from them.

Chapter Thirteen

Lalee's Betrayal

Maggie was right. The story was not over. Lalee's reaction at her kitchen counter when Makaila confronted her that first time and the question Lalee asked Maggie while laying in bed, in pain and sedated, were rubbing both Maggie and Makaila the wrong way. Something was not right. As hard as it was for them to admit and say out loud to each other that their mother was a liar it seemed to have a bigger impact on the mystery. Maggie didn't believe her mother, when she felt sorry for what they had gone through and when Lalee wanted to help... and Makaila didn't believe her mother when she said that she didn't remember anything about the Browns. Makaila and Maggie came to the conclusion that their mother did know something about what happened and that she was certainly involved. Mixed emotions played in their heads. Painstaking sadness enveloped them at the thought of what their mother was capable of doing... or what she did do. They felt angry that their mother didn't do anything to protect her girls from the Browns and pity for what their mother did to their father's life, their life and her own life...... and against God.

Father Ignacio contacted Makaila the day after his return from Mexico. It was a bittersweet reunion when he heard Makaila's voice over the telephone. He had wished and prayed that they were doing exceptionally well and hoped he never had to tell them what he believed may have happened to them. He prayed that Makaila would say that they had healed and had the love they deserve.

-- Makaila, Father Ignacio here.

Makaila almost dropped the phone. Her feelings of hearing Father Ignacio's voice after three months were confusing. Makaila felt somewhat abandoned by him and she further thought why she felt that he was supposed to be there for them. But hearing his voice made her smile and without knowing, her spirit rose within her.

-- Father, Are you back in town?

-- I am Makaila... Sister Angelica sends her regards.

-- Please tell her hello for me, Makaila said smiling.

-- Rest assured that I will, Father Ignacio told her.

-- I am so glad you are back, Father. I have so much to tell you.

-- I am glad to be back. How has Maggie been doing?

-- Not so good Father.

Father Ignacio's heart sank. He dreaded to hear that. He prayed and prayed that Makaila and Maggie were better than when he left. He didn't know how they would react to his fear about their past as little girls and why they had those memories.

Makaila hated to tell Father Ignacio that there was more to the memories that had already surfaced. Makaila felt ashamed and didn't want to impose on Father Ignacio what they had discovered. She felt embarrassed and unworthy of telling such a story, especially to a man of God. But a part of her felt compelled to tell him; that he must know the secret their mother was carrying and the new even more horrid memories they both were having.

-- What's wrong with Maggie? he asked concerned.

-- Well for one, she just got home from having surgery.

-- Dear Lord, is she okay? Father Ignacio asked.

-- Yes, Father, she is fine now. Makaila said almost under her breath. "But shortly after you left is when things got worse for both of us."

-- How so Makaila?

-- There were more memories Father.

Father Ignacio could hear Makaila's voice tremble through the phone. Could it be possible that they had remembered the worst? Was it possible that what he feared to tell them, they already knew? Father Ignacio needed to know; even though he already knew. "Dear Lord, how much more is there for them?" he thought.

-- Makaila could you meet me here at the church in an hour?

-- Father I don't know what to do? I'm sorry you have to deal with this.

-- Makaila? Meet me here in an hour.

-- All right Father, I'll see you in a little while, Makaila said as she sniffled and hung up the telephone.

Father Ignacio slowly put the phone back on the wall receiver. He stood there staring at the wall but not really looking at it. He retired to his bedroom for a quick talk with God asking for his guidance.

~ ~ ~

Makaila came over and they talked for a long time. Father Ignacio's soul jumped when the events of the past three months were told to him by Makaila.

Makaila told him about how Maggie saved her by remembering the subconscious memories.

-- Maggie was the one who called me and told me that she was having memories about the Brown's basement.

-- The same memories you both had three months ago? Father Ignacio asked.

-- No Father, different ones.

-- How were they different?

Makaila started to tear up.

194

-- Much worse than you can imagine Father. So much worse, Father.

Father Ignacio knew what she was going to say and he felt bad for her, but at the same time he was relieved that he wasn't going to be the one who revealed what really might have happened in the Browns basement. He was totally distraught about the revelation they experienced. He knew that those memories were coming from God in a perfect timing, in a perfect way, for a perfect reason...... but it almost killed him that they even had to experience that in the first place. He further thought, not only for what they remembered, but for what they have already gone through in their lives. The fear of the Browns, the torment of their braids being cut off and the association to something beyond their comprehension, their mother's slow deterioration due to alcohol and prescription drugs, their parent's anger and rages that came from out of nowhere, the safe people in their young lives disappearing, Bonnie's threats and evil innuendos, Maggie's illnesses and surgeries, Makaila's trauma surrounding basements and rats that she didn't have a clue about or the reason why, their suspicions of their mother and the constant mind set that their lives as children were all based on betrayal and lies..... and Father Ignacio knew that there was more to their memories and their last hope in trust for their mother. He felt that they would have to deal with something yet to come and Father Ignacio prayed for the day where the pieces to all their scattered memories would fit and that the story of their lives no longer haunted them into their future.

-- Do you want to tell me about it? Father Ignacio said with compassion.

Makaila burst into tears. She was so ashamed for what she was going to tell Father Ignacio, afraid that it would be too much for him to handle.

-- Makaila, tell me. I won't leave you. I will not abandon you.

Makaila was shocked to hear Father Ignacio say what she was thinking. Makaila felt even more blessed. Makaila's soul was touched. How she always wanted to hear those words and the sadness hit when she recalled that all she ever needed growing up was for her parent's words to match what Father Ignacio just promised her. And they did completely the opposite. She for the first time, apart from Maggie, did not feel alone in her fears. Someone was standing by her, supporting her and most importantly, believing her, and what a world of difference it made to have that feeling. Her soul and spirit were deeply touched. She knew God's hand was in this and she reached out and held tight.

-- Both Maggie and I have had identical memories.

-- What were the memories?

-- We remembered that in the Browns basement, we saw people carrying candles in dark robes, walking around in a circle.

-- "Oh, Jesus..." Father Ignacio said to himself.

-- and, and...... OUR MOTHER WAS THERE!!!!, Makaila screamed.

-- "Oh dear Lord," was all that Father Ignacio could say. His dreams and visions were right. How he wanted that they would not be. His knees felt weak. His head spun and he closed his eyes.

Father Ignacio grabbed Makaila and embraced her. Makaila fell into his arms.

Makaila's body shook with such force. Years and years of hurtful tears flowed. Father Ignacio's own tears made a track down his cheek. *"Blessed be the meek, for their reward in heaven will be great..."* He held her, comforting her, believing her and Makaila cried heavily.

Makaila felt heaven in Father Ignacio's arms. She felt that God himself was holding her. Her only thought was; *"he believes me, he believes me...."* and she knew that things were going to head for the best. She worried about Maggie and how Makaila wanted to take this feeling to her; the feeling of feeling safe, the love of God through Father Ignacio, and that of God's promise of not ever leaving them alone.

Makaila told Father Ignacio the details of their memories. Father Ignacio's spirit wept for them, for both Makaila and Maggie.... and Father Ignacio's soul poured out God's love and promises to them. Father Ignacio revealed to Makaila what they saw was a Satanic ritual, but assured her that they were safe in God's arms. And Makaila trusted him and believed for herself about God's protection.

~ ~ ~

Over the next several weeks, Makaila had so many questions for Father Ignacio and Father Ignacio answered her questions. Father Ignacio explained how the devil is a copycat, a deceiver, a ruiner of lives, but that God was much more powerful than that. He promised that goodness and right will always win victoriously. Makaila seemed to glow and have a lighter step after that, and Maggie was holding on to God's truth being revealed and Makaila still worried somewhat about her. Maggie still questioned their mother's accountability and just felt that it was not over. Makaila comforted Maggie, just like Father Ignacio had comforted her, and Maggie survived, they both survived and Father Ignacio remarked that these two woman were God's gifts to the world, and they were surviving spirits overcoming the worst.

~ ~ ~

Over the next several months, Makaila and Maggie met with Father Ignacio on a regular basis. The friendship between the three of them was special and unique. They often went to lunch or dinner and talking about their memories had diminished. Father Ignacio remarked on how much they had blossomed as women. Their lives seemed a little fulfilled now and they no longer kept in their subconscious that of which was weighing heavy on them. Makaila grew spiritually and Maggie even more so. Both Makaila and Maggie decided to join the Catholic Church and become members of the faithful. What an honor it was that they had decided to do that. Father Ignacio often prayed and asked for God's blessings upon the two of them and he himself was proud of doing God's work through Makaila and Maggie.

~ ~ ~

Over the next year, Father Ignacio transferred between parishes, and as always, Sister Angelica was part of that deal. Father Ignacio visited Monsignor Kealy a little more than usual and for different reasons. Monsignor Kealy was getting older and Father Ignacio worried that God would want him with Him soon. Fortunately, Father Ignacio's new parish was closer to Monsignor's residence, so it made visiting easier and more frequent. Makaila and Maggie went off in their lives and Father Ignacio always heard from them by either telephone or letters. Father Ignacio would never forget the work the Holy Spirit had done with their story and their connection with one another. Often, Father Ignacio would look up into the heavens and say, *"blessed be God... forever."*

~ ~ ~

Makaila called Father Ignacio one day, weeks after their last contact with each other and as always, they were happy to hear each other's voice. Unfortunately, the reason for calling was not a happy one. Makaila's and Maggie's father had died. Makaila seemed upset about her father's death but somewhat relieved. Makaila had always described her father as making her life crazy with things he wanted, didn't want, his attitude and personality and so forth. Both Maggie and Makaila requested that Father Ignacio keep them in his prayers as they headed home for their father's funeral. Father Ignacio knew that regardless about how her father was, Makaila would miss him and she did. Father Ignacio sent his condolences with her with an extra blessing for the two of them.

~ ~ ~

Makaila recounted the happenings surrounding her father's illness. She described how Jack worried how Lalee would be by herself. And as sad as it was for Makaila to see her mother, it really touched her to see the love Jack had for his wife. Makaila's only thought was, "what a fool he was....he could have had a much better quality of life if only he did not deny the extent of their mother's mental illness." But he loved her, there was no question of that and as hard as it was for Makaila to see, Lalee loved him, like she loved no other... and Makaila felt pity for her mother. She surely knew that Lalee losing Jack was as hard, if not harder, than when she lost her own father many years ago.

A month after the funeral, Makaila decided to visit Lalee. Makaila felt such compassion seeing her mother without their dad. Lalee was so lost without his controlling and protective ways; but Makaila still had problems accepting her mother's involvement with the Browns and Makaila thought it best to push that aside... for a while anyway.

This would be the first holiday without her dad and she felt that her mother shouldn't be alone for that. Makaila communicated with Father Ignacio that she was going out of town, but before she did, she explained to him this feeling that was enveloping her.

-- I feel that there is a rod between my mother and I that has been broken.

And the words that Father Ignacio said with such strong emotion and straight from God echoed in her head again as she heard this from him once before, and this time it took on a different outlook.

-- God is trying to prepare you for something, Father Ignacio said.

Makaila cried as she allowed God's presence to surround her..... and she really had no idea why she was crying. Father Ignacio confirmed with Makaila that he was only a phone call away, when and if she needed him. Makaila and Father Ignacio knew that they would talk again soon.

~ ~ ~

When Makaila arrived at her parent's house, Makaila felt a dark spirit about it that she had never felt before. Her soul jumped within her and Makaila made no mistake in what she was feeling.

A couple of days went by and she and Lalee talked about how much they missed Jack. Makaila did feel compassion for her mother. Lalee had always depended on Jack for most of everything and now, she was left alone to fend for herself and Makaila wasn't certain that she was capable of that.

They were sitting in the kitchen one afternoon. Lalee seemed agitated. Makaila wasn't certain for what reason. She thought it was because she forgot to take one of her many medications or because it was nearing her afternoon "drink." Lalee was playing with her pack of cigarettes, tapping its end on the kitchen table. Makaila remembered that Grandma Bella did the same thing. Makaila now felt that her mother was trying to tell her something. Without warning, Lalee spoke.

-- I am sure you won't mind, but I went to see my dear friend Mrs. Brown.

A bolt of lightening crashed through Makaila's body. Makaila staggered away from the table. Her heart felt as though it was pierced with a knife. She felt dizzy with such anger, such betrayal, such torment and anguish. Makaila felt as though she had died.

Makaila stayed in her room and hours went by into the middle of the night and Makaila felt like Jesus, praying in the garden. Makaila felt the ultimate betrayal anyone could have done against her and this person was their mother, again after so many years. No longer were the memories of the past haunting her, they were happening now and that was worse than any memory that had surfaced between Maggie and her.

Makaila laid awake most of the night. She developed a plan of what she wanted and needed to do. She prayed and God's presence and light filled the room. Makaila would confront her mother again..... and Makaila was afraid of what would happen after that.

Makaila knew that she needed to give her mother one more chance... one more chance to protect her girls, one more chance to be a mother, one more chance to hold them in her arms and love them... like they had always wanted to be. Lalee needed to align with her girls and that was the only way.

In the morning Lalee walked into the kitchen for a cup of coffee. She sat at the kitchen counter just like she had before the last time Makaila confronted her. Lalee acted calm like nothing ever happened the night before; a scene all too familiar to Makaila, a scene like so many times when they were children. Lalee was mean and drunk at night only to act differently the next day without a mention of what happened the night before.

Makaila felt God in her, through her and with her in a way she had never felt before.

-- You are wrong Mom, it does matter to me that you went to see Mrs. Brown.

Lalee's face transformed and in a voice Makaila had never seen or heard before, Lalee gruffly said; "She's my FRIEND!" Makaila unleashed everything she ever wanted to say. It had bottled up inside her. Makaila let her mother know about the Browns and there was no stopping her.

-- You mean you are friends with the same people who cut off our braids, tortured Maggie and killed animals in the basement?!!!!

-- She's MY FRIEND!!!", Lalee screamed in that same evil voice.

Makaila stood up and with God's words, strongly said;

-- I have loved you and you betrayed me.... you betrayed us. You have to choose.

-- I didn't touch her! SHE'S MY FRIEND! I choose them." Lalee said in an even more mean and evil voice.

Makaila felt like collapsing. Lalee had chosen Mrs. Brown over her twins. Makaila walked in a daze and the next thing she knew she was riding in a van headed for the airport. She didn't recall making a change to her plane reservation. Makaila sat in that airport shuttle van, completely dismayed. She left her mother alone, alone to align with the Browns, alone to figure out what she had done, alone to confront God and His wrath and Makaila felt like she was back riding in the Browns car, entrapped, only this time, she knew she was going home. Home with her mother was gone, the home she knew growing up was gone, the home where love, truth, peace were supposed to live, had been destroyed and Makaila would never go back again.

The anguish and feelings of abandonment were so intense for Makaila and Maggie came to her rescue.

-- I feel like I'm hanging by my nails on the edge of a cliff and I'm going to fall off, Makaila said in such grief and despair.

Makaila was not doing well emotionally. Her emotions were stuck in the Brown's basement like they had always been. Finally, after days of anguish and torment and the realization that God needed her to go on, Makaila finally broke through her emotions. She sobbed and cried so intently that her emotions finally broke through. She then realized, that she would live, because she had truly died inside emotionally. Makaila kept praying that if her mother died without coming back to them, Makaila would still have peace. Makaila truly felt that because she fought her mother's demons and stood up for God and God's victory overcame evil.

Father Ignacio was approached by Maggie about Makaila and even though Father Ignacio worried about Makaila's condition, he felt confident that God's plan reigned above it all. Maggie and Makaila both saw how tired and drained Father Ignacio looked, but no longer thought about it after they heard all the things Father had going on in his new parish. And Father Ignacio always had that perplexed look on his face whenever he prayed, or whenever he sensed something and this time, it was no different. Father Ignacio explained that their mother had to be alone with her demons and God would have to interfere in her life..... but Lalee had to do the work.

Over the next couple of weeks Father Ignacio and Makaila spoke. Makaila's love for God was stronger than before and Father Ignacio gleamed with that knowledge. Makaila kept Father Ignacio abreast on how they were both doing. Makaila told Father Ignacio about some things that had popped up about their mother. Things that Lalee had lied about all these years and the pieces were finally fitting and both Maggie and Makaila tried putting those same pieces together in their own lives.

-- Father... I can't believe it.... after all this about my mother... I still love her. and with deep love and commitment, the words that Father Ignacio said rang in her head like a loud bell, something she will never forget.

-- You have just experienced God's unconditional love.....

Makaila felt blessed. It comforted her knowing that God's hands were in this and was going to give her peace; and peace she needed. She grieved deeply over the reality of who their mother really was, the insane choices she has made in her life, how she sacrificed her children and how she had abandoned her twins for the next fifteen months. Neither Makaila nor Maggie had any contact with their mother and Lalee had no contact with them. To both Makaila and Maggie, the mother they thought they knew had died along with their father and Maggie and Makaila felt alone. They would never see their father ever again and as far as they knew, they would probably not see their mother ever again. God's unconditional love flowed between the two of them and with this they stood up for themselves, for what is right and good and they stood up for the glory of God..... still their hearts ached... closure to their story they felt had not happened and they waited for the day that God would wipe that feeling away.... they were confident about that, they had faith and Father Ignacio agreed....one day all of this would make sense.... all part of a divine plan... all part of God's protection and God's grace.... one day they would experience the fulfillment in their souls and then and only then would they know God's truth and their life and experiences would not and never be in vain.

Chapter Fourteen

The Return

Fifteen months had passed and neither Makaila nor Maggie had had contact with their mother. The months that followed that day in Lalee's kitchen, where she consciously chose to align with the Browns instead of her girl's, were slow ones. Both Makaila and Maggie thought that they would not see their mother alive again. They expected a call... a call that she had died and that was worse for them knowing that their mother was going to die without God's peace and forgiveness. God had granted them strength to go on and barely did they. They went on with their lives, feeling that their story was over... and as much as they tried going on with their lives, a bond, a tie, an invisible pull was still in their lives. They didn't know what it was or where it was coming from. They asked for God's command in breaking that and little did they know that it was God's plan for a job they needed to do for Him; an incredible job, a divine task, a heavenly intervention and that job was at hand.

Maggie did get a call that fifteenth month. It was their mother. The first time Lalee called, Maggie was dumbfounded. She felt that she had just talked to a ghost, a person that had died long ago. Twice Lalee called Maggie and twice Lalee tried to pull in Maggie. Maggie stood firm and told Lalee that she would not see her without Makaila. Maggie and Makaila promised each other that if their mother ever contacted them that she had to contact them together. They felt, *"where two or more are gathered"* would be their shield. Their faith had grown deeper through all of this but their grief was as deep as their faith. The phone rang in Makaila's new house.

-- Hello.

-- Makaila, mom's gonna call.

Makaila dropped to the bed.

-- What?

-- Mom's gonna call.... she has already called me. Whatever you decide, I will support it.

Makaila hung up the telephone. Makaila was both in shock and bewildered and amazed. She prayed on her bed. She prayed for whatever she needed to do, that she do without losing principle or losing sight of the reality of what their mother had done. Makaila paced the floor until her phone rang again.

-- Hello, Makaila answered knowing quite well who it was on the line.

-- Makaila?

Makaila just listened for a second. Her mother's voice was scarce, full of shame, and nervousness.

-- Makaila, it's mom.

Makaila's heart sank. Her mother's voice sounded so good to hear but yet Makaila could not deny the extreme hurt and sadness her mother caused her. They talked with one word responses as nervousness was obvious from both of them and their conversation seemed to be at a loss. Makaila prayed that she still had the courage to stand for her principles and she also prayed that her mother would have a different and a more right way of thinking. Throughout their conversation, Makaila brought up the Brown situation and what had happened the last time they were together. Makaila wouldn't let go of the torment the Browns caused in all their lives. Within their conversation, Lalee tried to skirt the issue of the Browns, until Lalee finally broke through.... she finally was able to talk about it.

-- The Browns had such a bad influence on our family. I'm so, so sorry.

Lalee's voice shook, sounded raspy, sounded old and frail. Finally, Lalee cried out of shame. Makaila cried with her. Through the rest of the conversation Makaila told her mother that she loved her and Lalee was genuinely shocked and amazed that she still did, that both Maggie and Makaila did. Makaila believed that it was the first time that Lalee believed in unconditional love and let it in. Lalee had love from their grandma, their dad and them, but had never received it openly. Makaila marveled how much she still loved her mother and knew that God was smiling in heaven because Makaila and Maggie imaged his likeness and being. After the tears were shared, the conversation went well.

-- Mom, what made you call?

-- I went outside one day and I looked up to God and said, "I want my twins back. Will you help me?"

Makaila teared up full again. She couldn't remember the last time she heard her mother talk about God or about talking to God. Makaila knew for certain that

God was smiling, bigger than ever.

-- I walked back inside and on the television were a set of twins, and I knew what I had to do.

God had intervened in Lalee's life that day.... all Lalee needed to do was to ask for help from Him and he would do the rest. God knew that Makaila and Maggie would be open in receiving their mother. That was part of their job and the rest of their task would complete the work God had laid out.... for Lalee had chosen her girls.

Maggie was coming out to visit Makaila in a week and Lalee asked Makaila if she could come along. Makaila said "absolutely!" and with that, Makaila and Maggie planned out how they would do that. Since Lalee lived in a different state than Maggie, Maggie would fly out to their mother's and they would both fly out to Makaila's together.

~ ~ ~

Lalee's many years of being a victim with secrets and lies had taken its toll on her, but despite that, Lalee still had a beauty about her.

They all three spent the best twelve days they had ever had together. They cooked and laughed and talked. Makaila and Maggie didn't care that it had taken this many years to feel that again. They just cared that their mother loved them enough to come back to them.

It was Sunday morning and both Maggie and Makaila were getting ready for church. Lalee asked if she could go with them. God smiled again and God knew His plan was taking place. Makaila knew that Lalee hadn't gone to church in a long time. Makaila secretly called Father Ignacio to let him know that he would meet their mother this morning. Father Ignacio praised God. Makaila had talked to Father Ignacio through these past twelve days and Father Ignacio felt a pride in Makaila. Makaila was attentive to the words of God, she had inclined her ear to His words and kept them close to her heart.

At the church, Lalee walked in timidly. She hung her head and Makaila held her mother tighter. Makaila only felt pride that her mother had again chosen, not only her girls but also God. Maggie decided to sit elsewhere since there were only two chairs available together. Through the beginning of Mass, Lalee just sat there. She looked around and hesitantly went through the motions. Lalee's body stiffened up, but she stayed there, and her heart had opened up.

When the congregation stood up to say the Lord's Prayer, Lalee recited after Makaila and took Makaila's hand. Makaila's body shook all over and Makaila smiled as God smiled. Makaila looked towards Father Ignacio at the sanctuary. Father Ignacio glanced over to her and to Lalee and he too smiled, and his soul jumped and danced in joy. Lalee continued holding Makaila's hand and tears fell down their faces. *"Our Father, who art in heaven, hallowed be thy name; thy Kingdom come, thy will be done......"* Lalee felt a release of emotions that she had never experienced before and Makaila felt it through her hands. The Mass continued as usual, they remained standing..... *"Lamb of God, you take away the sins of the world, have mercy on us,"* and Lalee fell her to her seat. Makaila bent over and looked into her mother's eyes.

-- Mom, God will forgive you, please ask for His mercy.

-- Not for the things I have done, she said shamefully.

Makaila smiled with tears streaming down her face.... "yes, He will." and Lalee did..... she asked for God's forgiveness. The light that shone around them, through them and on them, was so intense. Father Ignacio looked up at Makaila and the church lit up. Every window in the church shined its brilliance on them. Lalee turned to Makaila and asked if she could take communion. Respecting the rule of recieving communion for non-Catholics, Makaila prayed for an exception. She felt that God had permitted and insisted and with that Makaila's heart poured, her soul grew and her spirit warmed her.

-- Absolutely Mom!

They stood in line embracing each other and sobbed. Father Ignacio looked up and there was Makaila and her mother. Father Ignacio smiled, his eyes lit up.... *"The Body of Christ"* and Makaila said *"Amen!"* and took the bread. Father Ignacio turned his head to the right of Makaila, he looked at Lalee... *"The Body of Christ"* Lalee hesitated for a long time. Father Ignacio just smiled and it seemed that the whole world stopped and waited for Lalee to confirm, and finally, Lalee spoke the wonderful words God likes to hear. *"Amen..."* she said; and Father Ignacio, under his breath, said *"Amen"* as Lalee took the host and placed it in her mouth. Angels of God were flying everywhere. The sky opened up and heaven was smiling and streams of gold light shined everywhere. The choirs of heaven echoed their praises to God and it was felt by everyone. The people around Makaila and Lalee were crying with them. They felt it too. They came up and hugged Lalee and touched her hands, for they felt that she had been touched by the hands of God. Father Ignacio prayed silently and the praises of God were leaving his mouth to God's ears. It was so powerful as

when God spoke through Makaila when she said; *"I have loved you unconditionally and you betrayed me.."* and now Lalee was experiencing God's
unconditional love, something that Lalee thought she would never have and
this was His healing and Makaila was there to witness it. God had touched
Lalee's soul and spirit and had forgiven her and Lalee felt it. They all did.

A couple days before Lalee had to leave, they shared Bible verses and old
stories. On the day she left, Lalee held Makaila's face in her hands.

-- I love you Kare Kare.....

Makaila had completely forgotten that nickname that Lalee called her when she
was a child... and Makaila cried inside. She felt that she got the mom back that
she lost for so many years and now Lalee was at peace with God and her girls.

Lalee returned to her home and Maggie to hers. Lalee stayed in contact with
Maggie and Makaila. Lalee continued going to church and if she couldn't get to
church she would watch it on television. Makaila knew that their work was
done. The task God had for them was complete.... they brought their mother
back to God. The dream that Lalee had so many years ago, the dream that Jesus
asked her if she would *"take care of these two babies"* was in reality, *"will you
take these two babies... for they in turn will care for you and your salvation.."*
Father Ignacio had predicted the same thing when he first met Makaila several
years ago. He knew that they were born for a purpose, *"to bring back a soul to
God"* and now he, Makaila and Maggie knew which soul it was. God used her
twins, despite the hardship, pain and hurt to bring Lalee back to Him. For that,
both Makaila and Maggie felt blessed that He used them to bring their mother
back to life, a life with Him, a spiritual life and thank God she received Him.

~ ~ ~

Makaila and Father Ignacio celebrated Lalee's return to both Makaila and to Maggie, but ultimately her return to God. Makaila couldn't thank Father Ignacio enough. Makaila felt that their past and memories were over. All the pieces had fit together and the supreme purpose had taken place. Father Ignacio described that he had never experienced God's work in someone's life so genuinely as with Makaila and Maggie. He felt honored that he too was called onto the same mission. Everything made sense... things happen for a purpose and for a reason and we just never know how or why, but in this case, it was clear. God reigned supreme and that was all that mattered now. Father Ignacio knew that it was over. Their anguish, their memories, their pain, all served a purpose. A victorious purpose, and Father Ignacio was proud to be a part of that. Both Makaila and Father Ignacio felt the sadness in their hearts as they knew that this part of their relationship was over. There was no denying it. Father Ignacio would be transferred again. This time out of state. There were no long good-byes or visible tears. Father Igancio assured her that he would be coming back often as his order was stationed here; And they also knew that one day they would meet in heaven and that was enough for them. They looked back at the years that had passed and they talked about how they had each grown in so many ways. They knew they would see each other again as Father Ignacio promised he would be there when Makaila and Maggie were to be baptized into the Catholic Church as members. They departed with a long hug and a smile.

-- See you soon Father.

-- See you soon Makaila.

214

Makaila walked away.... she turned one last time and saw Father Ignacio standing there. His coat flapped in the wind and his hair waved gently. He smiled and raised his hand, Makaila smiled back and turned. Makaila kept her smile and the stream of tears rolled down her cheek. Father Ignacio nodded his head and made the sign of the cross with his hand over Makaila's direction.

~ ~ ~

On the day before their mother's birthday, Maggie dreamt that their mother had died. Maggie saw their father Jack pacing back and forth when Lalee showed up in the dream. Jack looked at Lalee, *"where in the hell have you been?"* and Lalee said, *"I've been trying to get here..."*

God had amazed them again when He brought their mother to Maggie's house and placed her in the loving arms of her twins.

Just before Christmas, Lalee called and asked if she could come down and spend Christmas with Maggie. Lalee also made plans to go to Makaila's after Christmas and spend time with her as well. Lalee hated flying but she was willing to fly alone. Maggie welcomed her into her home. They had as a grand time as the time they had at Makaila's. Their days were spent cooking, sharing recipes, shopping and eating soft pretzels with mustard. Makaila truly enjoyed hearing the fun they were having and couldn't wait for Lalee to come to her house.

Lalee wasn't feeling too good one day and thought she may "be under the weather" and Maggie made a doctor's appointment for her. Through blood work and tests, they found that Lalee was anemic and admittance to a hospital for a possible transfusion was inevitable. Makaila kept close contact with Maggie about their mother's health. Lalee did feel better and she was released and able to return back to Maggie's home.

-- For a minute, I thought I was going to be with your dad, Lalee mentioned on the car ride home.

-- You did? Well if you do, will you tell him I said hello? Maggie said.

-- That's the first thing I'll tell him, Lalee answered.

A couple of days passed and walking the stairs up to Lalee's bedroom, Lalee said with a calm voice; *"I think I'm on my last Hoo Rah."* Maggie thought, *"is she trying to tell me something?"* Even though Lalee felt better, it took only a couple of days where she felt ill again.

Upon hearing this, Makaila's intuition was flaring. *"She's dying.... am I nuts to think that?"* They both decided to admit her back in the hospital for more tests. That Sunday Makaila woke up with an urgency to go to Maggie's. She made a plane reservation and God worked His miracle again as Makaila bought the last seat available. On the flight to Maggie's, Makaila kept thinking that she had told her mother that she loved her, but not that she forgave her. Makaila arrived at 11:30 that night. She thought of calling Father Ignacio and because of the time difference, she decided to call him first thing in the morning. Makaila hailed a cab from the airport to take her straight to the hospital as Maggie had gone home since she was exhausted. They made plans for Maggie to meet Makaila in the morning.

Makaila walked into her mother's hospital room. Lalee was asleep. Makaila's eyes filled up with tears as she knew that her mother was not leaving this place alive. A nurse confirmed Makaila's fear.

-- She is dying. She has five hours or five days, but she is dying, the nurse sympathetically said.

Makaila's heart broke. Her tears ran down her face and onto her shirt. She remembered the last couple of months they had together and what a beautiful time it was. Makaila looked down at her mother, so frail, so sick, so ready to go home.

Over the next couple of hours, all Makaila knew to do was to sing her hymns like she heard when she was a child when her mother and grandmother and aunt would on occasionally sing before the girls were seven, before everything changed. Since Lalee was unconscious, it was Makaila's hope to reach her mother's soul. A couple of hours had passed by and Makaila knew that her mother's soul was restless. Again Makaila looked down at her mother and whispered in her ear, " *I forgive you... you need to let go now.... be with God and dad.*" Makaila began reciting the Lord's Prayer and the 23rd. Psalm.

-- Oh mom, you finally get to see your dad, Makaila finally said.

This was the father Lalee had so missed since his untimely death when she was only eleven years old, the father she finally admitted that he was not coming back when she was in her adult years.

Makaila laid her head down on the bed. It was 4:20 AM. A cool breeze went

through the room. It startled Makaila. Makaila looked up and her mother was
finally letting go. Makaila was there to feel the ultimate letting go and Makaila
knew that she and Maggie had walked her into heaven. Lalee died peacefully.

Makaila just stared at her mother who was now in the loving arms of her
husband and her father and God and Makaila also knew that Grandma Bella
would be getting a long awaited hug from her daughter.

-- You did good Mom.... I will miss you.... Makaila said as her final farewell.

The nurses came in shortly and Makaila called Maggie to let her know that
their mother was gone. After the exchanges of weeping, Makaila asked Maggie
to call Father Ignacio.

-- He won't mind if you call him this early. He would want to know. Makaila
assured Maggie.

In his bedroom, Father Ignacio's head tossed from side to side on the pillow.
Sweat glistened on his forehead and down his neck. He was having a dream, a
dream so real, a dream of a thousand questions.

*Outside was a restless night. The kind of evening that made every-
thing transient. The trees swayed, bushes rattled, dogs barked, cats
meowed and night time birds piped against the prevailing howling
wind that crept out of nowhere. The kind of evening that the full
moon, visible as that as the sun, illuminated all around. Out in the
distance a car horn blared, a muffled siren was heard. On an
evening like this, nighttime noises were muffled and nightime*

*scenes were blurred. Over the horizon, a light shone. A bright light.
Then it disappeared. Clouds rolled in and made their rest in front of
the moon. The blackness of the night enveloped its surroundings.
No longer were the crickets chirping, no longer were the frogs
calling. The symphonic music the tree leaves made, conducted by
the wind, ceased. Silence. Darkness. The earth began to spin. First
to the right, then a halt. Then it spun to the left and halt. again. The
bright light shined out in the distance. Gone again. The earth spun
again. A little further to the right this time, a little further to left as
well. Then it stopped. There again, the bright light... then the pitch
darkness. There in the darkness something moved. Standing in the
middle of this vast darkness was a figure of a man. Standing
straight he was, strong in his conviction. Strong in his purpose. He
was not disturbed as he focused on the bright light that would come
and go in the darkness. He reached out with his right hand and his
lips moved, though no sound left his mouth. Around him the wind
howled and blew stronger than before. Noises racked through the
air. The night has gone crazy. Complete and utter chaos surrounds
him. The man holds his stature firm to the ground as the tornado-
like wind tries to battle him down. The bright light flashed again.
This time closer. With every flash of the bright light, the man was
pushed closer to it. Then with a loud bang, the wind and noises
stopped. The only sound heard was that of the man's heart beat in
the night. As the man pulls his arm down, in the quietness of the
dark, a vision appeared before him. A single white door stood...
Unsupported by nothing but the darkness. The man stares trance-
like at it, still holding strong. Then the door swings out towards the
man and inside was complete darkness and sad muffled sounds were*

*heard. It stands open there for a few seconds then it swings away
from him in the opposite direction and the bright light that shone
before was there. The man instantly looks down, but his eyes still
gazes into the bright light. It quickly shuts. The door again swings
out into the darkness and back the other way into the light. The
door struggles with every swing as it were being pushed by forces
that could not be seen. Immediately, the door battles against itself.
Faster and faster the door swings to each side.... and in a moment's
notice.. it stops, swung open to the darkness. The noises were
louder, the cries even more distinct and sinister. Then BANG! The
door swings with every might to the glowing side. It swings with
such force that the door explodes. A strong gush of wind whirls out,
the man is forced down onto his knees. He keep his eyes at the
vision before him. The bright light envelops everything around him.
The door fragments whirl past him as he tries to escape from being
hit. It was then that he notices that the tremendous force of the door
exploding had changed the door. Right before him; the bright light
and a set of double doors are visible. The light is brighter than
before but he did not find it uncomfortable to stare into it. As the
man rises to his feet, he notices the peaceful breeze and the calming
sense of extreme happiness that he felt. Just then, someone lightly
touches his shoulder and calls out his name. He couldn't make out
who the voice was, but he felt he knew......*

- Father Ignacio?, Father Ignacio, wake up. There's a telephone call for you.
They say its important.

-- Thank you Sister, tell them I'll be there in a minute.

220

Father Ignacio, looked around his room. Still delirious to his everyday surroundings, he swipes his hand over his hair and yawns. He notices he is a bit drained from this wake up call; different than other times. Just then, Father Ignacio looked at his digital clock on his wooden desk that sat in the corner of his tiny bedroom that was too musty in the summer and too clammy in the winter. 4:32 AM. Who could be calling at this hour? What day is this?, Father Ignacio thought to himself. As he reached over for his robe, incremental pieces of memory from the dream he just had confused him. He knew he just had a dream but the only details of clarity that came to him were those of victory. He shook out his thought as he opened up the door to his bedroom and walked down the hall of the rectory. There Sister Angelica stood, with a cup of hot coffee waiting for him at the kitchen table. Father Ignacio smiled at her a smile that had seemed to have said, "thank you, thank you Sister. Where would I be without you."

Father Ignacio picked up the receiver, held it close to his ear, took a sip of coffee,

-- Father Ignacio here.

-- Father?

A distinct sniffle was heard on the other line. Father Ignacio could not make out who the person was apart from being female.

-- Yes, this is Father Ignacio

-- Father, I hate to wake you up at such a late hour. But my sister asked me to call. She said that you wouldn't mind.

-- Oh, Maggie, yes. Is everything all right? Where is your sister? Is she all right?

-- Yes, Father, she is fine.

-- What's wrong Maggie?

Maggie was quiet for a minute.

-- Mom just died.

Father Ignacio told Maggie that he should be there shortly. Father Ignacio hung up the telephone, ran his fingers through his hair and brushed his brow. He took another sip of coffee as he sat there. He peered out into the garden of the rectory. He rose, cinched up his robe and walked out into the crisp air. Memories flooded his mind. Memories of when he first met Makaila. Memories of many talks, walks and laughter. Memories of the incredible story that unfolded before him. Memories of two spirits that survived.

Chapter Fifteen

The Calling

The flight to the hospital was a particularly short one, or so it seemed to Father Ignacio. He thought of the numerous times he and Makaila talked about her life, her memories, her mother, Maggie and their survival. He had watched Makaila grow stronger with each day, week, month and year that passed by. He again thought of the woman who invited him to coffee when they first met at the workshop he was presenting at the University. He praised God for how He worked in their lives and had brought them together for the salvation of one special soul. Both Makaila and Maggie, through the tears, the heart aching pain they endured, their horrid memories, the suffering they went through as little girls and the suffering they journeyed through again as adults, survived the unbelievable, survived ultimate evil, survived life. And now, their work as servants, as unique gifts to God, had sealed their deal with heaven. Their mother was on her way there. Evil did not prevail, Satan did not have a soul, the Browns did not win. It was because of God's plan that these little girls brought their mother to her knees, received and accepted love unconditionally, accepted God as her King and asked for forgiveness. It was these two little girls that defeated what evil wanted. It was these two little girls that opened the doors of heaven and showed their mother the way there. It was these two precious blond-haired, blue-eyed, little girls that made it possible for their mother to hug her father, to hug her husband, embrace her mother and feel God's breath..... for eternity.

He prayed that Makaila and Maggie accept their mothers' passing, knowing that they were instrumental in her salvation at the perfect time.

Father Ignacio arrived at the hospital shortly after nine o'clock that morning. He was dropped off at the loading and unloading section of the hospital's main entrance. He walked into the hospital and headed towards the information desk, visible from where he was standing. He smiled at the elderly lady manning the information desk and asked for Lalee's room. After some slow directions from the woman, Father Ignacio walked towards the elevators up to the floor number given. Father Ignacio smiled at everyone that entered the elevator, others shied their eyes away as not to stare, at the "priest." But the majority of the time, people seemed warm and pleasant.

The elevator doors opened up onto the floor marked. Father Ignacio stepped out looking for the room number. He glanced from left to right reading the door numbers and the names below it. He found Lalee's room. He took a breath and walked in. Both Makaila and Maggie sat at opposite ends of the bed. Makaila on the left of their mother and Maggie to the right of her. They were both holding their mother's hands and with their other free hand they held onto each other's. They had tears in their eyes but a smile to their lips. Lalee looked as all beautiful as Makaila had always described her. Father Ignacio noticied how she even looked different from the first time he saw her at communion that one special day. A peaceful, more content look was on Lalee's face and Father Ignacio was convinced that she was dancing through the clouds of heaven. Maggie looked up and noticed Father Ignacio standing at the door. Her eyes full of tears and yet a bigger smile broke through. Makaila looked at Maggie and Makaila turned around to see him standing there. A tear rolled down her cheek as she jumped up and grabbed his hands. Father Ignacio smiled at her, *"I am here, Makaila...."*

-- Father, thank you for coming, Makaila said pulling back a sniffle.

Makaila let go of his hands and hugged him.

-- How are you Makaila?

Maggie got up and walked over to them. Father Ignacio hugged Maggie.

-- How are you Maggie?

-- We are fine Father, and Makaila acknowledged the same.

-- We are really fine, Maggie finished. "thank you for coming," she added.

-- I wouldn't be anywhere else, Father Ignacio responded.

Makaila and Maggie held onto Father Ignacio... one on each side of him. Father Ignacio thought to himself, "How could anyone want to harm these women? How could anyone want to hurt the little girls they were? They are the example about what being in love with life is about. They are both caring, empathetic, generous, funny, charismatic, loving, honest.... and Father Ignacio realized, "that's why!" Makaila and Maggie stood for everything that was right. The reason why they tried separating them, the reason they thought of killing them, or hurting them, the reason they thought of doing away with them, was because they were going to be their downfall. The downfall of ruining innocent lives for eternity, the downfall of everything that's evil, the downfall of the Browns.

-- She looks peaceful, doesn't she Father? Makaila asked looking at her mother laying in her hospital bed.

-- That she does, Makaila.

-- Father, do you think she made it to heaven? Maggie asked.

Father Ignacio looked at the two of them.

-- What does your heart tell you? What do you feel?

Makaila looked at Maggie and Maggie looked at Makaila, their tears flowed gently down their cheeks and they knew that Lalee had made it. Father Ignacio walked over to Lalee. He smiled and whispered to her, "I am so proud of you." He looked at her for a moment, then he raised his hand up and over Lalee's head and blessed her. Makaila's and Maggie's hearts were touched as they heard Father Ignacio's Latin benediction upon their mother. They felt honored, blessed that they had such a wonderful man in their lives. A man who had journeyed with them in their shoes for the past five years, a man who did not abandon them, a man who believed them and stood next to them in battle...... this man..... their friend.

The hospital nurses and staff walked in a few minutes later. They had to take Lalee and Makaila and Maggie had to start the funeral arrangements. When Lalee was being wheeled down the hall, both Makaila and Maggie held on to Father Ignacio and their sobs and tears came freely, but there was no remorse, no regret....and as sad as it was for them, they were much happier for their mother.... and happy for God.

After some immediate paperwork at the nurses' station, Makaila, Maggie and Father Ignacio headed for the elevators down to the hospital cafeteria. They stood in line making idle chitchat, looking at the menu, even though knowing all they wanted was something to drink. They looked around the cafeteria tables and found a table by the window that overlooked a beautiful flower garden and waterfall. They all sat. They looked around the cafeteria, both Makaila and Maggie did and Father Ignacio thought they expected their mother to walk in.

-- Are you both really okay? Father Ignacio initiated the talk.

-- We really are Father, well I know I am, Maggie would have to answer for herself.

-- I am fine too Father, really. I am feeling quite at peace and accept mom's passing. I'm fine.

-- That's good to hear. You know, that both of you are quite remarkable women, he said positively.

-- Thank you Father, but I don't see how..... Makaila said until Father Ignacio cut her off.

--I know, I know for certain that you both were instrumental to your mother coming to terms with what she had done.... and she did ask for forgiveness.

-- Yes, but.... Maggie started saying.

-- There are no questions.... It is absolute. You two were instruments in one of God's big plans. Do you know that when your mother was dying this morning, I know now what she was fighting, Father Ignacio said.

-- Fighting? Makaila questioned.

-- Yes, she was fighting in letting go.

-- You know what Father, right before she died, I felt that her soul was restless. It was that way for awhile. Makaila said with an amazed look on her face.

-- Maggie, right before you called... I was having a dream and on the flight over here, I remembered what the dream was. You see, I dreamt that there was this light that would shine so bright and all of a sudden it would be pitch black.... when I got closer to take a look, I saw that a door was swinging back and forth and every time the door swung to one side, a bright light poured out of it, but then it would swing back and when it did, there was complete darkness.

Makaila and Maggie swallowed every word that escaped Father Ignacio's mouth. Makaila and Maggie just sat there, hearing what Father Ignacio had to say next.

-- The door was fighting itself. It trembled every time it stayed on one side too long.....then the door exploded into the light side.... and the amazing thing is that the door changed.

-- It changed? How did it change? Maggie asked.

-- The single door became two doors side by side and it was open and the light that came from beyond that blinded me in the dream.

-- Father, what do you think it means? Makaila finally asked.

-- The dream was about forgiveness, Father Ignacio said calmly.

-- I don't think I understand, Maggie said and Makaila nodded in agreement.

-- The light represented good, right and God. The darkness represented bad, wrong and evil. Your mother was battling good versus evil. She was the single white door.

-- She was still deciding about where to turn to? Makaila asked almost quiet-like.

-- No, she was fighting forgiveness.

-- But she asked God forgiveness. God didn't forgive her? Makaila asked almost tearing up.

-- No, God forgave her.... Father Ignacio said smiling. He waited a few seconds before he spoke again, "She didn't know if she could forgive herself........ That's what the battle was."

Makaila and Maggie started to sob. What their mother must have felt like after the realization what she had done in their lives and in hers, must have been terrible.

-- She finally forgave herself. .... and the only reason she forgave herself was because of you two.

Makaila and Maggie looked at each other with tears in their eyes.

-- You two were the double doors that led her way to God's arms. She let go and she finally accepted the unconditional love you had for her.

-- Oh Father, what a dream, Makaila finally said through broken words.

-- There is one last thing, Father Ignacio said, lifting his cup of coffee to his mouth. One thing I noticed was that the doors, rather it was the single door or the double doors, was that they were all white. God was always going to prevail anyway. It was His promise. It all makes sense now.

They continued talking for an hour or so and they convinced Father Ignacio to stay at Maggie's instead of a hotel. Makaila and Maggie were pleased that Father Ignacio was going to stay for the services. Makaila and Maggie privately talked about Father Ignacio's dream and they felt good about it. They felt a certain amount of sorrow for what their mother went through in order to forgive herself, but they were confident that it all was worth it to her, just for the chance of being with the men she loved and the mother she was able to finally receive love from.

~ ~ ~

The services for Lalee were beautiful. Glorious flowers filled the funeral chapel and pictures of Lalee were visible throughout the front of the chapel.... and the music was glorious as they sang, "How great Thou art, and Amazing Grace." Makaila and Maggie felt like their mother was joining in on the music being sung..... and Makaila and Maggie left the services fulfilled that the last piece to their story was put into place. Their story had finally ended.

~ ~ ~

On the last day before Father Ignacio had to leave, he told Makaila and Maggie that there was one more thing he needed to do before he could go. He asked Makaila and Maggie to take him to the house the Browns used to live in.

Makaila and Maggie didn't know what to think, but they trusted Father Ignacio and so they complied. They all three prayed together at Maggie's house before they left and the ride to the Browns house was a quiet one. Father Ignacio knew when they were close to approaching the house. His soul within him stood guard and his spirit prepared for battle.

Maggie pulled the car to the curb in front of the Brown's house and Father Ignacio asked her to park the car further up. Father Ignacio jumped out of the car and headed up the driveway to the Brown's house. Makaila screamed after Father Ignacio, only Father Ignacio ignored her. He walked slowly up the driveway. He turned to Makaila and Maggie and instructed that they stay there in the car. Every step closer to the house was getting heavier for Father Ignacio. His breathing was getting faster and his movements tighter. Pictures flashed in his head. Pictures and visions, of the basement, candles, dark robes, the upstairs, Bonnie's bedroom, the stove, the wooden door, an ax, a paddle, a rifle, a table, blood, rats, the hidden door in a closet, the dark living room, the refrigerator, the tool shed, and the garage. All these images popped into Father

Ignacio's head. His heart beat faster, his hands were clammy and his forehead shined of sweat. He heard evil laughter and evil sounds, horrid screaming and yelling. Father Ignacio felt the flashes of pictures pierce his arms. He turned to look at the front door. A vision played in his head. He saw Maggie running up the steps of the basement in slow motion, her eyes were wide and her mouth gasped for every bit of air she could get. With every step Maggie made she looked back as if something was behind her. She opened the door of the basement and ran down the hall through the house. Maggie ran and ran, continuing to look behind her, she came to the front door and desperately tried to open it. Maggie looked back and back at the door, the door crept open and Maggie ran outside. She didn't look back this time. Maggie smiled as she saw her twin sister standing on the front steps of the porch with her hand extended. She looked back one more time and with all her might she jumped off the porch and grabbed Makaila's hand. They smiled as they both looked back... and they never looked back again as they skipped down the sidewalk ....hand in hand. Only Father Ignacio didn't see the little twin girls, he saw them as they were now... as adults.

Father Ignacio's vision stopped as quickly as it came. He started walking backwards down the driveway. Evil faces peered out of every window of the house, evil sounds got louder. Father Ignacio stopped. He looked at the house and with a strong mind and a conviction in his voice, said; *"You've lost!, It's over... You will never have the twins, never. God has been victorious... again.... and always will be!"* He took one step back... *"You weren't strong enough, you never were."* Father Ignacio turned his back and walked down the driveway. Makaila and Maggie were staring at him the whole time he was up there. He got into the car quietly and without a word about what he saw or experienced. Maggie started the car and drove off and not one of them looked back.

Makaila and Maggie felt different since then. A completeness overshadowed them. Makaila and Maggie insisted they drive Father Ignacio to the airport, Father Ignacio accepted.

At the airport, Maggie hugged Father Ignacio. She looked deep into his eyes and their souls touched.

-- Thank you, Maggie said smiling.

-- It has been my pleasure, Maggie, Father Ignacio responded.

Maggie pulled back and let Makaila in. Makaila hugged Father Ignacio for a long time and whispered in his ear, "what would we have done without you?" and Father Ignacio replied, "what would I have done without the two of you?" Makaila held Father Ignacio tighter. Maggie stood in the background and tears rolled down her face. The terminal loudspeaker announcing the departure of Father Ignacio's flight was heard. Makaila let go of Father Ignacio, tracks of her tears visible on her cheeks. "We will see you soon right, Father?, Makaila asked. "absolutely Makaila, see you soon." Father Ignacio replied smiling as he turned and walked down the jetway and out of sight.

~ ~ ~

Two weeks later, Father Ignacio called Makaila. The news he had for her was not good but, could not be helped. Makaila's and Maggie's baptism into the Catholic Church was unfortunately on the same date that Father Ignacio had to go out of the country on a Pilgrimage with the Bishop. Makaila was of course disappointed but completely understood. Father Ignacio promised them that he would take them out to dinner one night after their baptism to celebrate. He would call later that Sunday afternoon to go over the details.

-- See you soon Father.

-- See you soon Makaila, Father Ignacio said smiling and with a smile to his heart and soul.

Makaila and Maggie were nervous wrecks that morning of their Baptism. Mass had started and the music and the ambience of the Easter Sunday celebration was soul and spirit touching. They held hands throughout the Liturgy and they smiled like they never smiled before. They still wished Father Ignacio was there with them, witnessing their conversion, but they were more than pleased knowing that their mother was smiling upon them from heaven.... and they knew that Father Ignacio had already sent thousands of blessings upon them this day.

The moment came when Makaila and Maggie were going to be baptized. The priest stopped and leaned into Maggie and Makaila.

-- Father Ignacio sends his blessings upon you, the priest said. "Father Ignacio insisted that you both be baptized together. It is his wish."

Makaila and Maggie smiled at each other and tears rolled down their faces, and with another priest present their baptism began and in unison both priests raised their hands full of water and poured it over Makaila's and Maggie's heads saying, *"Makaila and Maggie, we baptize you in the name of the Father and of the Son and of the Holy Spirit."* They both closed their eyes and marveled at the brilliant light that entered their body. They felt the love of God in their heart and could feel God's breath on their faces. Their souls danced in unison and their spirits sang out praises. They both felt Father Ignacio standing there with them and they smiled forever. It was Sunday April 14th, 11:55 in the morning.

~ ~ ~

Makaila and Maggie would never forget that day and the feeling they hadthey carried in their heart forever. They truly felt that their story was over and nothing was ever going to take them back there. They felt that they could finally close the book and tuck it away, never to be opened again.

Father Ignacio didn't call that day like he said he would. Both Makaila and Maggie wanted to share with him the experiences they felt. They waited another day for Father Ignacio to call, but he didn't. Makaila decided to call Sister Angelica.

-- Hello?

-- Sister Angelica? It's Makaila, How are you?

-- I am fine dear.

-- Has Father Ignacio returned from his trip yet?

-- Oh, my dear.... Her voice cracking a bit, "Father Ignacio was called home."

-- Home? Home where?

-- Father Ignacio died on Sunday, I'm so sorry, my dear. I was going to call........

Makaila dropped the phone. Bursts of cries escaped her throat. Maggie came running from the back bedroom. *"What, Makaila!! What?"* Makaila fell to her knees, holding her head in her hands. *"Father is dead, Father Ignacio is dead!"* Maggie staggered back in disbelief. Tears flowed from her eyes onto the carpet at their feet. Maggie sat next to Makaila on the floor and they cried and held on tight to each other, rocking each other in comfort, sharing each other's grief.

~ ~ ~

The day of Father Ignacio's funeral, Sister Angelica walked Monsignor Kealy into the church where the casket of Father Ignacio stood. They came in an hour early before the ceremony. Monsignor Kealy could barely walk as grief of Father Ignacio's passing had taken its toll on his body. Sister Angelica walked him slowly towards the casket placed in front of the altar. The church smelled of the sweet fragrance of freshly cut flowers. The Sanctuary Lamp glowed it's color over the altar and onto the casket. Flowers lined the entire Sanctuary area and on either side of Father Ignacio's casket. Candles filled in every other space in between and the glow of their light lit up the altar as if looking onto God's throne. Monsignor Kealy approached Father Ignacio's casket and as frail and slow, Monsignor genuflected at the front of Father Ignacio's body. He bowed his head towards the Tabernacle and finally looked down at Father Ignacio. His old eyes filled up with tears as his mouth quivered.

-- Nachito, my boy, he said barely making out the words. "I dreaded for this day to come. I shall miss you."

Tears rolled down his wrinkled cheeks, his eyes red from the tears he shed. He reached into his pocket and took out a book. The same book, Father Ignacio saw at Monsignor's house. Sister Angelica reached into her pocket and took out another book. The same book that Father Ignacio had in his safe and accidentally left out. They were identical books. Monsignor Kealy opened up the book and removed a page from it. Sister Angelica handed Monsignor Kealy the other book. Monsignor Kealy opened up that book ever so slowly and inserted the page he removed from his book. He slipped his book with the new page into his coat pocket and the other book he slipped under Father Ignacio's hands. A tear rolled off his chin and landed in the casket.. Sister Angelica fought the tears that welled up within her. Sister Angelica slipped her hand underneath Monsignor Kealy's arm and helped him to his feet. Monsignor Kealy looked into the casket one more time.

-- Rest in peace.... Father Ignacio.....

And with that Monsignor Kealy turned around and walked ever so slowly down the aisle of the church. Sister Angelica followed behind him, giving Father Ignacio their final procession.

~ ~ ~

Makaila and Maggie attended the ceremony at the cemetery. They had done all their grieving before and now only smiled within themselves for Father Ignacio. As people started walking away after the ceremony, Makaila and

Maggie stayed behind. The day was beautiful and they remembered how Father Ignacio would turn his face in the direction of the soft wind and close his eyes and smile. The wind that blew that day was gentle and their white dresses waved against their legs. They turned their face in the direction of the wind and smiled. Maggie stepped forward and placed her rose on the casket and whispered, "thank you," and walked away. Makaila brought her rose up to her lips and gently kissed it. She placed it on the casket, she smiled as a single tear left her eye.....

-- See you soon Father....

and in the wind that muffled by her, she could hear,

-- See you soon.... Makaila....

and Makaila smiled.

~ ~ ~

Father Ignacio sat on a rock underneath a large shade tree that overlooked the ocean. His hair waved gently in the wind. He lifted his face in the direction of the wind and closed his eyes and smiled. He then slowly tilted his face back down. He opened his eyes and marveled at the ocean before him against the bluest sky he had ever seen. He took in a deep breath and let it out ever so slowly. He rose to his feet, stuck his hands in his coat pockets and turned to walk away.

-- Makaila? Maggie? he yelled.

-- Coming Father.... was yelled back.

Father Ignacio stood in a field of wild, yellow daisies and out in the distance, with a hand full of daisies, were two seven year old little girls, dressed in pink and white dresses, blue-eyed, blond-haired with a pink bow at each end of their braids. They held hands as they skipped towards Father Ignacio.

-- Are we going now Father?

-- Yes we are Maggie

-- and Father, where are we going again?

-- We're going to a wonderful place, Makaila.

-- and what's going to happen to the other Makaila and Maggie who live on earth?

-- Oh, they are older now, they will be just fine, Maggie.

-- Tell us again, Father, who we are.

-- Well, we are spirits, Makaila.

-- Have we always been spirits, Father?

-- Well not really Maggie, you see, the other Makaila and Maggie saved you and set you free and here we are.

-- Have you always been a spirit Father?

-- Well Makaila, I have always been with you two. I was your strength and your faith...... I was your soul and you two were mine..... and now, we are three surviving spirits and right through there.... is home.

Makaila and Maggie smiled at each other. Makaila held onto Father Ignacio's right hand and Maggie held on to Father Ignacio's left and they walked towards the direction of the sun. Father Ignacio was finally bringing the twins home..... and the twins were bringing Father Ignacio to the same place. Their work was done.... heaven acquired three more souls..... and God smiled.